Sometimes I Look at Sinners

Sometimes
I Look at Sinners

A Collection of Short Stories

GLORY S. DAVIS

DavGlo Publishing, LLC

SOMETIMES I LOOK AT SINNERS

Copyright 2014 by Glory S. Davis
DavGlo Publishing, LLC
27372 Highway 21
Angie, Louisiana 70426

Cover design by: *www.wordzworth.com*
Book design by: www.wordzworth.com
Copyediting by: Professional Book Editing

Library Congress Cataloging

ISBN (paperback): 978-0-9914475-0-3
ISBN (ebook): 978-0-9914475-1-0

Manufactured in the United States of America
First Edition

I dedicate this book with love to my family

First, to my sons,
Terry K. Jefferson and Thomas L. Davis;

Second, to my grandchildren:
Tyriah, Terry K., Savion, Toi 'Cora, and Jai 'Nyla;

Third, to my sisters and brothers:
Helen Banks, Shelly Babers,
Georgia Robinson, and John Banks.

Last, to all my nieces, nephews, and cousins,
who are too numerous to name.

Acknowledgements

I thank, posthumously, my mother, who implanted within me a love for learning and my father who taught me the value of hard work. Without their solid foundation, this book would be impossible.

The Author

Contents

ONE

The Landlord's Glass Houses

When Rachel walked across the yard to her landlord's house next door, she was determined. She was going to tell Salina, the landlord's wife, that she was pregnant from her husband, and she wanted him to recognize her child as one of the Johnsons. However, when she got to the house, she could not muster enough nerves to tell Salina. So, she decided to postpone revealing the father of her child until later. And, as an excuse for coming, Rachel pretended that she had come to pay the rent.

"I thought I'd come and pay my rent before I spend it," Rachel said.

"Good," Salina, told her, "We need to start saving. I haven't told Charley yet. In fact, you are the first to know. I am pregnant again, and we need to start saving for the baby."

Rachel paid her rent and went home dejected. She could not tell Salina now that she was pregnant from her husband. What good would it do? Telling her now would do no good at all. Earlier, when she left home to confront Salina, she was full of hope. She thought that if she told Salina about her pregnancy, maybe, she would leave Charley. Now that Salina was pregnant, too, Rachel knew that her chances were destroyed. Salina, pregnant with her third child, would never leave her husband.

At home again, Rachel considered her next move. She decided that she would tell Charley that she was pregnant. After all, they had made the baby together. He, not Salina, should decide how to solve this little problem.

When Charley returned home from buying groceries in downtown Roseland, he paused and looked at his property before he went inside the house. He was proud of himself. He had managed to escape the shame of sharecropping, had saved enough money to buy some land and build a decent home, and after a while , had built a little rental house next to his own to help support his family. In doing so, he had earned the respect of the community leaders and the church, in a small town where respect was priceless and gossip was destructive. "What more can any poor man want in this town in '63," he smiled as he unloaded the family's groceries and looked toward the rental house hoping to see Rachel. He had no idea that his little secret was boiling, bubbling out of control and his whole life – wife, home, rental house, and community respect – was in danger of imploding.

Salina unpacked the groceries and put them away. She noticed that Charley had not bought the Oscar Mayer bacon or the Aunt Jemima syrup she wanted, but instead had bought some off-brand that neither she nor the children liked. Nevertheless, she said nothing to Charley about it. She knew that it was better to accept whatever he brought home. She had learned long ago to over-look a lot for the sake of peace.

When she had put everything away, she gave the rent money to Charley and asked him for a few dollars to buy some cloth to make Lena, their oldest, a dress for the school play.

"Money for a play!" he shouted. "We can't waste any money on such foolishness."

"Lena is doing so well in school," Salina pleaded. "We need to support her all we can. Many of the other 12- year-old girls are doing absolutely nothing in school."

"No," he said, "we can't waste a dime. I need this money to pay bills." As usual, Charley put the money in his pocket and gave her nothing. He was not about to; for, he had other things to do with that money. And, it didn't include Lena, little Charley, or her for that matter. And, as usual, Salina gave up and allowed Charley to have control. She had done it – given him control – in everything all the years of their marriage. He did all the shopping, paid all the bills, and controlled all the family's money. All she did was cook, clean house, and follow Charley's directions. She had always been the submissive, obedient wife who was very careful to maintain peace in the family.

So without protest, Salina dropped the request for a few dollars and went into the kitchen to prepare dinner. She made Charley's favorite – fried chicken, mashed potatoes, green beans, and sweet potato pie – because she wanted him in the best mood possible when she told him about the baby. When she thought the time was right, she said, "I have some good news."

"What is it?" Lena asked excitedly, "Am I getting the new dress?"

"No", Salina told her, "This is good news for the entire family."

"Well, what is it?" Little Charley asked.

"Oh, go on and tell us," Charley said.

"I found out today that I am... going to have a baby. Lena, you and Little Charley are going to have a little sister or brother."

The children were happy, but not Charley. He looked at Salina as if she had stolen the family's fortune. "A baby," he said, making sure that he had heard her right. "We are having another child?"

"Yes, we are," she told him. "Aren't you happy?"

He said, "Sure," but the frown on his face and the stare in his eyes told Salina that he was definitely not happy about bringing another child into the world.

At four a.m., Rachel turned the alarm off and lay in the darkness, fully awake. She listened, not for some creature's cry to disturb the night, but for Charley who usually came at that time two or three nights a month. She knew that he would knock three times as a signal, that he would come, as always, expecting sex, and that he would return the rent money that she had given Salina. That was their plan: sex for rent. For a while, the plan seemed foolproof. Salina never suspected anything, and the neighbors didn't have a clue.

Charley knocked as usual and Rachel let him in. "I thought that you would never come," Rachel told him as she closed the door behind him. "I have something very important to tell you."

"What is it? I sure hope it's not bad news. God knows I've had enough of that tonight."

"Charley, I'm pregnant."

"Whose is it?"

"It's yours. I haven't been with anyone else. You know that. What are we going to do?"

"There is not much that we can do. Salina told me tonight that she was pregnant. I have to take care of my family."

"What about me? What are you going to do to help me?"

"I told you. There is nothing I can do right now. Here," he said as he gave her the rent money that she had given Salina, "this is the rent money for this month. It should help until we can figure out what to do."

Unlike other times, Charley and Rachel did not have sex that night. They were too worried about their situation for that. Instead, they spent the rest of the time together trying to figure out how they were going to keep Salina from knowing that Rachel's baby was his. At first, he told her to say the baby was his brother's child.

"No," Rachel told him. "That would never do. Your sister-in-law, Nancy, is crazy. She just may kill your brother and me. We have to come up with a better idea."

"Why don't we wait," Charley told her. "You aren't showing yet. We have plenty time to figure out what to do. Salina doesn't suspect anything, and she won't if we are careful. You have been careful, haven't you?"

"Of course I have. Salina thinks I am her best friend. I told you that I am deceitful, conniving, and bitchy, but I am not stupid. If Salina find out about the baby and us, it won't be from me."

"Good, I'll see if I can get someone to own the child." Charley told her as he slipped out of the back door into the darkness.

Charley arrived home at 5 a.m. unnoticed. Salina and the children were still asleep and, as always, had no idea that he had left the house during the night.

He did not go back to bed. Instead, he stayed up trying to think of a way out the mess he had created. He felt sure that he could continue his fling with Rachel if he could only get someone to say that he was the father. He thought of several single men that he could approach, but dismissed them all because he just couldn't trust them. Most of the men he knew couldn't keep a secret.

"But, what if I paid them to cooperate, I bet I'll get someone then…, and he'll keep quiet." Charley said as he began to sort through his friends again, trying to find one that he could give a few dollars to cover for him. He settled on Darnell "Slick" Smith. Charley knew why people called him "Slick." He was the kind of person that would do anything for money – even sell his own mother. He was sure that he could get Darnell to pose as the father and act as a go-between for him, if he gave him enough money.

"Now, let me get this straight. You want me to say that I am the father of Rachel's child," Darnell repeated to be sure that he understood what Charley wanted. "Why?"

"Well, the real father is married, and his wife is pregnant too. He wants to keep his family intact. And, he doesn't want to lose his sweet thing. In other words, he wants the best of both worlds. As a result, he is willing to pay someone to act as the father so that he can keep both.

"Are you that man?" Darnell asked just to hear him say it. Charley wasn't fooling him. After all, he was "Slick." Darnell had already figured out everything. He knew that Charley was the father, that Salina was pregnant, and that Charley was desperate. He also knew that a desperate man would pay plenty to keep such a juicy secret.

"Yes, I'll do it," Slick said, "What's in it for me?"

"Two-Thousand, that's a good figure," Charley told him.

"It's a good figure only if you are going to pay all the expenses for that baby." Slick was quick to say.

"You won't be out of anything. I'll handle all the expenses." Charley told him before considering all that he was taking on.

"Then, I'll do it." Slick said and sealed the deal with a big smile.

Charley paid Slick the $2,000 and told Rachel about the deal. "What do you think about it?" he asked her one night. "Do you think we can trust him?"

"I don't know," she smiled, "with a name like Slick, who knows?"

Charley and Rachel were skeptical, but they could think of no other choice. They put their fate in Slick's hands and prayed for the success of their little scheme.

Slick did a good job of posing as the father of Rachel's child. He worked true to nature. First, he casually mentioned to his friends that he was dating Rachel. Later, he made sure to visit Rachel at times when the nosiest in Roseland would see him there. Then, before she start showing, he parked his car in her yard and left it there overnight to make people think that he was staying there. As if that was not enough, on Valentine's Day, he ordered – in full view of everyone in the store – a dozen roses, had them delivered to Rachel, calling out her name and address loud enough for all to hear.

When Rachel reached the eight month of her pregnancy, Slick passed out cigars. "My job is done," he said. "Everyone, in Roseland is fooled. I'm Finished." To close the deal, he approached Charley with a final bill.

"A final bill," Charley said, "I thought the $2,000 was the final payment."

"Remember the expenses," Slick told him. "You promised to handle all the expenses."

"What kind of expenses do you have?" Charley asked him.

"You owe me for the roses, the cigars, the nights that I parked my car away from home, the damage to my reputation, and the other gifts that I bought..".

"Wait a minute," Charley said, "I am not paying for all of that."

"You will if you want your secret kept," Slick threatened.

The threat worked. Charley reconsidered. He remembered that his relationship with Salina had improved since he was not spending so much time with Rachel. He also remembered the church and how he had been ordained as deacon the week before. He surely didn't want the pastor to find out about his little secret sin.

"You've got my back against the wall," he told Slick.

"No, you've gotten your back against the wall. If you weren't such a snake, you wouldn't be in this situation," Slick yelled.

"Well, if that's not the pot calling the kettle black!" Charley shouted. "Man, how much do I owe you?"

"Another $1, 500," Slick said.

"C'mon, $1,500! You listen! I'm going to give you this money! But this is it! This is all that you are going to get!" Charley told him.

Charley was wrong. Slick came back several times, and several times Charley gave in to him. However, when he was out of another $2,000, he decided to end his fling with Rachel for good and find some way of getting Slick off his back.

The next night, he told Rachel that she had to leave. He gave her two weeks to clear his property. "I've gotten in too deep and need to find some way to crawl out," he told her. "No one knows your baby is mind. It's my word against yours and Slick's. Everyone will believe me.

"I won't be coming back," he told her as he slithered out the back door and disappeared in the night.

Rachel was furious. She paced the floor, trying to figure out what to do. "I'm not going to let him get away this time," she said, more determined than before. "Oh no, he is not going to get away with this! He is no better than I am. I will not let him live happily in his glass house, as I shatter to the ground in this one."

She dressed and left the house, intending to go next door to expose Charley. In the darkness, she tripped on a stone or a limb and fell to the ground. At that moment, her water broke. Struggling in labor pains, she could not turn back or go forward; she lay there needing help. Desperate, she gathered all the strength she could and cried out in fear. "Help! Help! Somebody help me!"

When the Johnsons came out of their house to see what was happening, Rachel was unconscious on the ground, and the baby, a boy, was lying is a pool of blood, strung to her.

"Hurry," Salina said, "Let's get them inside." Together, Charley and Salina managed to get the two into the house. Charley cut the cord, slapped the baby on his butt, and was relieved when the child cried out. Salina took the baby from Charley and hurried to the bathroom to clean him. When she returned with the baby all cleaned and passed him to Rachel near her husband, she gasped in anger.

Rachel never got the chance to expose Charley. The baby did that. He was a mirror image of his father – same beastly eyes, same big nose, and the same baldhead.

TWO

Now, Run Tell That

Cousin Hannah bent down, picked another handful of cotton, and stuffed it into her sack, which was already bulging. When she stood again, she was at the end of her row and saw, as usual, the other workers were trailing far behind her. "Lord, Lord," she said, "am I going to have to do this every day?" She then changed her full sack for an empty one and crossed over to Linda's row next to hers, and she began picking on it towards her. When they met, the two crossed over to the next row. Hannah picked toward the end while Linda picked toward the worker. When that worker's row was finished, the three crossed over and helped the next worker finish his row. This teamwork continued until all the workers were at last at the end and ready to weigh-up for the day. Most accepted the practice of helping others as norm among share-croppers in the early '60s, and very few complained. However, Cousin Hannah had had enough. She decided that something must be done. "A change," she said, "needs to come to this farm soon."

At home that night, Cousin Hannah `complained to her husband Buster that the slow workers were not pulling their share of the load. "I don't know what I am going to do, but something must be done," she said. "I am 65, my arthritis is getting worse, and I'm so tired when I get home at night that I can hardly make supper."

"If you lose some weight, maybe you want hurt so much at night," Buster told her smiling.

"My weight has nothing do with my being tired. Those lazy cotton pickers you hired keep me working long after I finish my last row for the day. Anyway, I don't weigh but 195."

"Now Hannah, you know that you are 250 pounds and not a pound less. You need to stop lying so much. You can lie about your money, you can lie about your children, but your weight is one thing that you can't lie about. One look at you will prove you a liar."

"That's it! That's what I'll do!" Hannah said to herself.

"What are you talking about?"

"I am going to get some work out of those lazy boogers."

"How are you going to do that?" Buster asked.

"You'll see," she said. "You'll see."

The next day at the cotton patch, Cousin Hannah got her cotton sack, selected a row next to Laura, the slowest of all the workers. She knew that Laura was slow because she was nosy, always stopping to listen to some gossip and to put her two cents in. "Laura," Cousin Hannah laughed. "Let me tell you what happened to me last week."

"What happened, girl?"

Cousin Hannah picked faster and Laura bucked down to

be sure to keep up and not miss a word. "Well, I discovered that someone was stealing from me."

"Stealing from you, what did he take?" Laura picked a little faster to catch up and to hear because Cousin Hannah was almost whispering.

"I had $30 on my dresser that I was saving to pay the rent."

"Did they take it all?"

"No, they didn't take it all."

"You mean to tell me that you had $30 and the thief didn't take it all," Laura said as she picked a little faster because Cousin Hannah was going top speed.

"Come on, girl. Listen to this! I thought it wasn't nobody but Buster."

"Your husband? Well, was it him?" Laura said as she hurried to be sure not to miss a word.

The other workers who were at least 15 feet behind began to pick a little faster for they wanted to hear what on earth Cousin Hannah was telling Laura.

"Hannah, what did you say happened to you?" John called out ahead to her.

"I just said that someone was stealing from me."

"Stealing from you?" John asked as he rushed to catch up. "Who do you think it was? What did they take?"

"Part of my rent money," Hannah said. "But, I set a trap for him."

When old Georgia, who had stopped to rest after only 30 minutes on the job, heard the word trap, she immediately sprang up, buckled down, and began shortening the distance between Hannah and her. She did not want to miss a word, and in no time, she was neck- and- neck with the storyteller questioning her about the trap that she had set. "Well, what did you do?"

"The next night," Hannah said, "I put $50 on that same dresser and lay down before Buster. I played 'possum, for I was determined to catch him in the act." Before she went on with her story, Hannah stood, looked around, and saw that her scheme was working. All the workers were up close to her, and they were about to finish the first round of rows without having to help anyone else with their pickings.

"Well," two or three of them asked at the same time, "did you catch Buster?"

"No."

"For God sake, Hannah," Terry questioned her impatiently, "What on earth happened?"

Pulling to the end of her row and making sure that the others were doing the same, Hannah told them that she lay in the dark with one eye opened and one eye closed for about 30 minutes. "When the crook thought that I was sleep," she said, "he tiptoed in and took $5 off the dresser."

"Who was it?" The workers questioned like a well- directed chorus.

"It was Sonny, my youngest, looking like a hungry puppy stealing a bone."

"What did you do?" John asked.

"What could I do? It was my baby. I rose up and told him..."

"Told him what," Georgia asked.

Cousin Hannah smiled and said, "I told him to put the $5 back and get that $10."

Aaah! Everyone sighed disappointedly as each selected new rows and started a new round of picking. They joked about the incident, and Terry asked her several times, "What did you tell him, Hannah?" She would then smiled, hold her head back, put her hands on her hips and say, 'I told him, put that $5 back and get that $10." And, all the workers would break out in laughter again. Soon the laughter stopped and the workers slipped into their old habits.

Thirty minutes later, Cousin Hannah looked behind her and saw that the crowd was lingering back again. "Hey," she called back, "have y'all heard what happened to Amos and Tom?"

"Who's Amos and Tom?" Shelly asked picking a little faster to catch up and not miss a word.

"Them boys that Betsy and Jack took in as foster children last month."

"I saw them when I was at Betsy's the other day. I didn't know who they was. Boy, she had them strong out... mopping, dusting. I bet they have never worked so hard in their lives. What happened to them?" Shelly asked as she picked a little faster.

"Well, Betsy and Jack killed a hog," Hannah said mysteriously trying to make the others interested in her story.

"I know," Shelly said. "They sent me the liver. Did they send you anything?"

"No, I kinda wanted the chitlins, but they kept them for themselves."

"What happened with the boys, Hannah? What does this hog killing have to do with them?" Shelly asked trying to get to the point about the boys.

Cousin Hannah picked faster as she told them her second story. According to her, Jack and Betsy killed a hog that Tuesday morning. They thought that they would have time to string it up, gut it, and clean the chitlins before prayer meeting at 5 o'clock. They miscalculated and had to rush to get ready for church and get there on time. They left Amos and Tom home with strict instructions to clean the chitlins before they returned. One thing they did not consider, however. They never once asked the boys if they knew anything about cleaning chitlins, nor did they tell them how to do so. They thought that the boys were from Campti, Louisiana, not far from Coushatta. "Everyone – man, woman, and child – within a 40 miles radius of Coushatta knows how to dress a hog and clean chitlins," Betsy told Jack as they left for church.

By the time Hannah got to that point in her story, all the workers were picking alongside her, and they were impatient to get to know the end.

"What did those boys do? Did they know how to clean chitlins?" Shelly asked.

"Of course not, those boys were really from somewhere up North, near Shreveport or Monroe," Hannah said Laughing. "Dey had never seen the guts fresh out of a hog," she said smiling and went on with her story. "To kill the odor, Tom poured pine oil on them. When that wouldn't do, he got Betsy's new gallon of Clorox bleach and poured all of it on them. When Betsy and Jack opened the door returning from church, the smell hit them. The shit from the chitlins, the pine oil, and the bleach made quite a stink. Both Jack and Betsy covered their noses and yelled, 'What's that smell?' When Tom told them that he was soaking the chitlins to get the smell out, Boy, all hell broke loose!

"What did Jack and Betsy do?" Shelly asked just to see what Hannah would say. She knew those two – Jack and Betsy – first hand and she knew those boys definitely would not get off easy for destroying such a delicacy. Why, Betsy had been known to be mean, real mean.

Hannah paused pretending to collect her thoughts. What she really was doing was trying to think of something to make her story interesting. "Well," she went on, "Betsy grabbed the first thing she saw – a frying pan – and hit Tom in one eye and then the other with it so hard that black circles ran around his eyes and made him look like a panda bear."

"My God, what did Jack do?" someone said.

"He pulled Betsy off Tom and did his best to calm her down." Hannah said as she pulled her sack off and rushed toward the bushes on the fence row.

"What ya doing?" Shelly called out to Hannah as she disappeared out of sight.

"I got to use it! I got to use it!" she said. "I'll be right back! I'll tell y'all the rest in a minute."

While Hannah was gone, the workers discussed her story. Sally had seen the boys on Wednesday, and nothing was wrong with Tom's eyes. "Hannah must be lying," she said. "There is a new law – passed in January. It is against the law to beat your children. If that story was true, Jack and Betsy would be in jail."

At first, the other pickers did not believe her. "You mean to tell me that you can't beat yo own children," Shelly said in disbelief.

"Naw you can't," Sally assured her. "Three men were arrested in Shreveport last month because they beat children. And, they's still in Jail. If you don't believe me, ask Mr. Bill when he comes to the field."

Mr. Bill was the white landowner. All the black folk knew that if they were told to ask him, Sally must have been telling the truth.

When Hannah returned, Sally asked her about the child protection officer of which Hannah knew nothing. But, not knowing did not stop her from lying. She stuttered, put two and two together, figured that the child protection officer was supposed to help children, and continued to entertain the workers...

"Oh," she said, "you mean that woman... err, err... Mrs. McLamore. She. err... err... heard about Tom and went to Betsy's unannounced. When Betsy saw her coming, she hurried up and told Tom to tell her that he ran into the corner of the house."

"But he had two black eyes. How did they explain the other shiner?" Sally asked just to see what lie Hannah would tell.

"Well, according to Betsy," she told them, "He got one black eye when he ran into the corner of the house, bounced back, fell, and hit the other eye on a rock." That story was unlikely, but most of the workers, except Sally, believed it.

Sally knew Hannah was lying, and she did not like it that she was lying on her dear friend, Betsy. I can't wait 'til quitting time, she thought. I am going straight to Betsy's and tell her what that lying Hannah said.

She did just that. When she was dropped off at her house after work, she did not go inside. Instead, she walked a mile, as tired as she was, to Betsy's house. "I came over here to tell you what Hannah is telling people about you and Jack," Sally said as she sat in the nearest chair to rest.

"What she's been saying?" Betsy asked feeling anger slowly boiling inside of her. "Jack," she called out to him, "come in here so you can hear what that lying Hannah been saying about us." When Jack came into the room, he saw the anger in his wife's face. Even he did not dare to cross her when she had that look. He moved hesitantly to her side, and Betsy asked Sally, "Now what has that witch been saying?"

"She is telling people that you beat them boys and gave one two black eyes. When the child protection officer came, you made the boy lie to her… told her that he ran into the house."

"I can't wait 'til tomorrow," Betsy said. "They'll see who has two black eyes. They'll see."

"I got to go now," Sally told them. "I didn't take time to go inside the house – Came straight here 'cause I thought ya'll should know. It's a shame for people to be lying on good church folks."

When Sally cleared the house, the boys came into the room. And, sure enough, neither had a black eye. Betsy asked Jack, "What if child protection gets a wind of that lie… they'll be in here trying to take those boys from us. Oh yes, Hannah's gonna pay for that lie." She snarled as she clinched her fist. "I'm gonna pay her a little visit tomorrow." At first, she decided to wait until the workers quit in the evening. On second thought, though, she knew that would take too long… all day long. "No," she said, "I am going to meet her where she told the lie."

Betsy got up early the next day, put on her work clothes, and left walking toward Buster's cotton patch. "Why don't you wait," Jack called out to her. "Somebody will be by here soon, and you can catch a ride."

"No, I can walk there in 20 minutes," Betsy yelled back to him.

When Betsy arrived at the field, the other workers were already busy. And, Hannah held them intrigued, telling then about a ghost that she said she had seen in her kitchen the night before, playing with her mixing machine. Before Hannah could tell the rest of the story and what she did to the ghost, Laura saw Betsy coming across the field toward them. "Something must be wrong," she told them. "Here come Betsy, and she doesn't look too happy."

Hannah rose up from her picking, saw Betsy coming without a sack, and immediately knew the reason for her visit. "Somebody musta told her," she said. "Now what am I gonna do."

Betsy didn't say a word to the workers... not even good morning. She just stalked on toward Hannah with that look of revenge on her face. When she was within 10 feet of her, Hannah flashed a wide smile, showing all her teeth... trying to defuse Betsy's anger. "Hey, girl," she lied; "finally got you to come to dis ole cotton patch. Wanna help me out with my row while I tell you how I tricked the workers into keeping up and how I tricked you into coming to work." Then, as if she was trying to fool Mr. Bill, or some other white man, Hannah laughed and laughed -and laughed, slapping her thigh all the while.

"Don't you try to bullshit me . . . you... you liar! That mule won't work today," Betsy advised her. "Lying is just bad... plain bad. And, when it hurts someone's reputation, it's the work of the devil – down right evil. If you want to get the workers busy, why don't you... WHISTLE!" At that, she swung a left hook to Hannah's right eye and then a right hook to her left eye, knocking all 250 pounds of her flat on her back. Then Betsy put her hands on her hips, looked down at Hannah and snarled, "Now, run tell that!"

THREE

The Test

Jesus, sitting on the throne just right of God, wondered about the fullness of time. He checked the heavenly calendar and saw that it had been over 2000 years since He last walked the earth as a man. Two thousand years should be enough time, He thought. But, I am not sure. I need to test to see if the people are right and ready for judgment. But, how could He perform such a test? Jesus decided to go to the earth in person to see how the people would react to Him.

When He told the other members of the Trinity, God and Holy Spirit, what He wanted to do, they reminded Him of the last time that He was on earth as Himself. "Don't you remember what they did to you" said God. "They crucified you for God's sake!"

"Yes, they rejected you and even your own disciples denied and ran away instead of helping when you were crucified," reasoned the Holy Spirit.

"That's it. I want to see if the world has changed any," Jesus said, with enthusiasm in His voice. "If at least 90 percent of the people that I encounter prove true to me, then we can at last celebrate the Day of the Lord. My father, don't you want to see Satan defeated? Hasn't he caused enough havoc on our people?"

God thought for a minute. He remembered His dislike of Satan, how he had caused a civil war in heaven, how he has fooled and stolen so many of His angels and people to his side, how he has caused hate and discord in the world for so many years. At last, He decided, why not? Why not give it a try? When He looked at Holy Spirit and back again at Jesus, He saw that, as usual, they were in perfect unity – all three agreed to perform the test. God said simply to Jesus, "Go!"

When Jesus landed on earth, He found Himself in South Louisiana with a tough decision to make. "Where should I go first – to the church, to the world or non-Christians, or to the government?" He whispered, as He considered possible choices. After much thought, He chose to visit His own first; after all, most of them are called by His name and had praised Him and worshipped Him for years. Surely, the church would definitely recognize and welcome His return.

Like a Genie re-entering her bottle again after a while of roaming from it, Jesus nodded His head twice. On the second nod, a whirlwind appeared, scooped Him up, and carried Him to the small town of Varnado, Louisiana. When it stopped, it was hovering above Mount Sinai, a Methodist church who had often boasted of being a church with opened doors. "This is a good spot," Jesus said. "Let me down here."

Outside of the church, Jesus decided that He would change into something more modern and abandon His long white tunic, His sandals, His turban, and His staff. On second thought though, He said, "If I am not dressed as I have been pictured for years, they may not recognize me. I had better not change."

Jesus entered with a group of late comers, and because there were parishioners all around Him, He was not immediately noticed. However, when the usher had seated everyone except Him, He stood in full view, and – like on a movie screen in a country theatre – all eyes were on Him.

Sister Johnson, sitting in her favorite seat, three pews from the front, eyed Jesus in disgust. She leaned over and whispered to Sister Banks, "What the hell!"

To which, Sister Banks whispered, "The nerves of him coming in here disrespecting our Lord. Something ought to be done. This is blasphemy!"

Sister Cole, in her attempt to quiet them and be logical at the same time, whispered, "Maybe we are having a drama today."

All three ladies checked their programs simultaneously and found that there was nothing unusual or special scheduled in it. They kept up such a commotion with their whispering that the usher near them leaned over and asked if they could be a little quieter. It was then that the pastor stood and announced communion, thinking that it, the most sacred part of the program, would restore order. He was wrong. Someone in the back yelled, "Preacher, you have skipped recognition of our guests. We have visitors in our midst." The pastor paused awhile but recanted and asked all visitors to stand and introduce himself or herself to the church.

When it was Jesus' time to speak, He said very distinctly, "I am Jehovah Shammah, the Lord present with you. I am on a mission to test the readiness of my people. I want to see if the world is ready for the fullness of time."

"Did he just say that he was Jehovah?" Sister Georgia said loud enough for everyone to hear.

"He must be crazy," someone accused, laughing.

"Excuse me," the pastor said. "Who did you say you are?"

"I am Jesus Christ, the son of God. I am I Am, and I am here to initiate the beginning of the end." That did it!

Brother Leroy, thinking that we indeed had a lunatic on our hands and that we were about to witnessed an incident like the Sandy Hook massacre, eased out through the side door, and phoned 9-1-1. He told the receptionist that a lunatic claiming to be Jesus was in church at Mount Sinai on Jones Creek Road. "Send someone out here quickly," he shouted. "We need help! He said that he was going to end the world! We need help!" He repeated.

In no time, a SWAT team was there. By the time that they rushed through the doors though, Jesus had gone to the pulpit, had taken the tray of wine from the altar, and was saying, "Come, drink; this is my blood."

"Grab Him!" The officer schemed.

"What is wrong, Sir? I am Jesus. I am just helping with the Lord's Supper."

"Yah, right," the SWAT team commander said sarcastically. "And, I am the Lone Ranger! Get down on the floor!"

When He didn't move immediately, Jesus was wrestled to the floor, put in a strait jacket, and dragged out of the church. All the while, He kept repeating: "I am Jesus; don't you recognize me! I am Jesus; don't you recognize me!" Sadly, no one did, not even Pastor Jones.

After Jesus and the SWAT team all cleared out of church, the pastor commended Brother Leroy for his quick thinking and thanked him for perhaps saving lives. Brother Leroy beamed with pride. He, nor any of the others, realized what had really happened. They had literally thrown Jesus out of His church.

Two blocks from the jail, Jesus decided that He did not want to waste time there. He realized that if He were booked into Jail, He could be held indefinitely waiting for someone to recognize Him. After all, His church didn't. They certainly would not come. He had not planned to, but He decided that He had to use His powers if He was going to complete His test. So, He nodded His head twice. And, just like before, a whirlwind appeared, scooped Jesus up, and whizzed Him away.

In a blink of an eye, Jesus was hovering over New Orleans. This time He decided to test the non-Christians. "Take me," He said, "to Bourbon Street."

Thinking that His clothing may have added to His problems before at Mount Sinai, Jesus decided to change into something less noticeable. A pair of jeans and a Saint's tee shirt replaced His outerwear; a pair of Jordan sneakers replaced His sandals. And, when He noticed that everyone was carrying a cell phone, he blinked an eye and an iPhone 5 appeared in His hand. Getting rid of His staff, He was ready to test the city called "The Big Easy."

It was Mardi Gras in New Orleans and thousands of tourists and native Louisianans were out celebrating when Jesus appeared on upper Bourbon Street that night. He was amazed at all the opportunities for harvest that He saw there.

There were strip bars, gay bars, and novelty shops all reeking of drugs, sex, and alcohol. Speaking of alcohol, almost everyone was carrying at huge drink of it; – if not a Hurricane, they had a large Hand Grenade. He saw prostitutes dressed in scanty costumes showing much too much almost everywhere. One even propositioned Him, but He quickly shouted, "Away with you Satan," and she disappeared out of His sight. Another beckoned Him to her. When she looked into His eyes, she ran for her life – maybe she, like the devils of old, feared Him and wanted no dealings with Him.

At last, Jesus, already troubled by what He had seen, wandered into the Big Easy's Blue Light Club. If He had not known better, He would have thought that He had stepped back in time and was entering the ancient city of Sodom – or Gomorrah. Sin was rampant. Strippers were dancing nude on stage, and homosexuals were kissing in plain view, drunks were lying on the floor; drug dealers were soliciting customers in front of Him: these were just few of sins that put Jesus into a trance. And, He saw His people the way they were before the Babylonian exile. In every corner, at every table, on all of the faces, He saw the devil mocking Him, whispering to Him, "I am winning; I am winning!"

Anger consumed Jesus, and He decided to destroy the city. He raised His hands to summon His thunderbolt. But, before He could say "to hell with you," He felt a crushing blow to the head, felt His warm blood streaming down His face, and felt His legs buckle underneath Him. He was being mugged. The robber took His Jordan sneakers, His iPhone, and His Saint's tee shirt and ran out of the club. He quickly disappeared into the crowd of revelers. Jesus, determined to see if someone would come to his aid, lay on the floor waiting... waiting... and waiting....

No one came – not even the bouncer who witnessed the whole scene and acted as if the robbery was a common occurrence. Neither did the bartender who continued to serve customers even though Jesus lay bleeding a few feet away from the bar. And, the customers went about their dancing and drinking as if nothing had happened, as Jesus lay there losing consciousness in the midst of hundreds who could have helped but did nothing.

When Jesus was almost lifeless and crusted over with His drying blood, God, the Father, looking down from His throne in Heaven, knew that He had better intervene. For, man, lost in his sin, would not. He sent Gabriel, the archangel, to Jesus' aid with a message telling Him to end the test. After Gabriel had revived Him and cleansed him, he delivered the Father's message. Jesus was disappointed. "End the test," He said. "But, I haven't visited Congress yet. I want to see how the government will respond to me. And, I need to speak to them."

"Congress is in session now," said Gabriel, "we can detour there. But, I caution you that it might not be safe to walk into Congress."

"I'll use my powers if necessary. And after all, you will be with me. Let's go to the House of Representative first; they seem to be the most religious," suggested Jesus.

Making themselves invisible, Jesus and Gabriel walked pass the guard at the front gate, pass several House members on break outside of the door to the main chamber, and walked into the House. They found seats in front and sat down in full view of the Speaker. When they materialized, both were wearing their long white tunics, mantles, and sandals – typical of Eastern wear. The Speaker, examining their clothing, immediately guessed that they were terrorists. However, he did not cry out or cause a stir. Instead, he wrote on a note pad, "Get help quickly. We have terrorists on our hand. This is serious. Help!" He gave the note to a doorman and watched him rush away toward security.

When he called the House to order, Speaker Boehner was horrified. He feared that those suicide bombers just in front of him would detonate bombs at any minute and kill all of them. So, he said nothing when Jesus walked up to the podium, but he nervously watched for help to come rushing through the door. Some of the members eased out; however, others – out of curiosity or ignorance –stayed to witness what would happen.

At the podium, Jesus identified Himself as Jesus Christ the Lord, and told them that He was the Way, the Truth, and the Life. "I have come," He said, "to see if I could end the world and establish my kingdom as promised. However, I see that it's not time, yet. If I end the world today, too many will be lost. And my original plan for salvation will be defeated. Therefore, I just want to warn you to flee from the wrath to come. You have made laws that have hurt the least of my people. You have failed to protect the most venerable among you. You have let greed consume you, and you have not kept my commandments. You have rebelled against the leader that I set before you – at a high cost to the well-being of this nation. Worst yet, you have sinned and rebelled against me. If you do not mend your ways, then I will destroy the world with fire beginning with this House. I destroyed the world once; I will destroy it again. Flee from the wrath to come!"

Before He returned to His seat, the House security stormed onto House floor with their rifles pointed at Gabriel and Jesus. "Hold it right there!" One of the officers shouted. Jesus, thinking that this must be a mistake, made a step toward the officer to explain. All hell broke loose, and the SWAT team fired – emptying all their rounds into them. But they were no match for Jesus' power and Gabriel's divinity. Together, the two formed a giant whirlwind and left through the roof, leaving all the members baffled.

In Heaven again, Jesus met with the other members of the trinity and reported His findings. He told them of the problem He had encountered at Mount Sinai and of how they did not recognize Him. He described the sin He had witnessed in New Orleans, the blow He had received, and His near-death experience. And, He explained why He had spoken in the House – to warn the world of the wrath to come. The three decided that it would take some time yet before the world reject sin and come to know Him. "It's sad; it's sad," God, the Father cried. He paused, collected Himself, and continued. "It would best to erase the memory of your visit from minds of all those you encountered." And, with a wave of His hand, He did just that.

FOUR

Confessions of a Fool

Baby, (she called her granddaughter Baby even though she was 30.) 'there's not much to tell about me. I confess... I've been a country girl all my life. Sharecropped with my dad, left home and went to college, graduated and taught for almost 45 years, outlived two husbands, and now I am a loner at 79. Good thing you come by to see me every month; otherwise, I just might die of loneliness out here in Colfax." She smiled and sat in her old rocker near the fireplace.

"Why don't you visit the Senior Citizens' Center? You can get involved in a lot of activities there. Since granddad died you've done nothing but sit around this house," Tyriah said concerned that her grandmother might be getting a little senile since losing her husband six months before.

"I can't stand to go there... nothing but a bunch of nosy, old ladies. I'd rather stay here and watch TV alone than to be bother by them."

"Well," Tyriah said, "I worry about you here alone," and she walked near her grandmother to give her a hug. Before she had a chance though, she noticed a picture on the mantle that she had never seen before. It was of a young soldier, maybe 20 or 25 years old, standing near a draped American flag. The picture had worn on the edges and had faded with the years. Picking it up, Tyriah said, "Grandma, who's this? I don't think I've ever seen this picture before."

"No, you haven't. I put it away long before you were born. It's been locked in a trunk for years. I found it the other day when I was looking for some quilts... I've been real cold at nights lately. I took it out and set it there."

"Is it one of my cousins?" Tyriah asked wondering why her grandmother had it locked away. "...He must have been special to you?"

"He was," she said, and went on to tell her granddaughter a love story that was somewhat like the picture – old and secretly tucked away in her memory for years:

'I loved him... for as long as I can remember, he has been the center of my thoughts, even throughout two marriages. I doodled and daydreamed about a happy life with him. And, I don't think anyone – not my husbands and nor my children – had any idea that I harbored a secret love all those years.

'I shall never forget when I first saw him. He was the new boy on campus at Springville, and I saw him from my seventh grade classroom window. ... must have been 1959. 'Who's that,' I asked Alice, my best friend. She told me that he was Thurston Bernard Jackson, the boy that Mr. Nelson and Nancy Washington took in. She thought that he was from somewhere down south, maybe Breaux Bridge. She told me that he had just enrolled in the fifth grade in Mrs.

William's classroom. He's cute, I said, and I didn't see him anymore that day.

"When I went with my mom to prayer service on Tuesday night, there he was, not with the Washingtons but all by himself. He stayed two doors down from the church, and the Washingtons had allowed him to walk to the meeting alone because it was safe back then. Deacon Smith introduced him to the congregation, and we all welcomed him to Colfax. From then on, I went to church regularly – Sunday school, BTU, choir practice, communion service – because I knew, he would be there. My mother didn't have to convince me to go to Mt. Zion Chapel; I begged her to take me. And, from a distance, I slowly fell in love with him. Ah, his positive attitude, his politeness, his crew cut, his neat, preppy dress, and his sweet, slanted smile: all charmed me into a world of dreams.

"I was an eighth grader when he first asked if he could phone me. Of course, I said yes. After all, I had been in love with him for almost a year. I gave him my phone number, and he said he would call me after school. Home that night, every time the phone rang, I dashed for it. After a call from the preacher for Dad, a call from Alice about homework, and a wrong number, I thought he would never call. The phone rang again, though. And, Dad answered and handed me the phone. His voice on the other end said, 'Flora?' I melted and felt my legs trembling under me as my heart skipped a beat. Not wanting to sound ignorance or too anxious, I steadied myself and very properly said, 'This is she.' We talked for what seemed like hours.

"I told him my age – then 13 – and my birthday, July 23. He was also born in July – on the first of the month. Our birth month was not the only thing we had in common. We were both on the honor roll, both active in schools clubs, both members of the same church, and both loved reading. He read about the sports – all of them: football, baseball, golf, and hockey. I, on the other hand, loved reading **Modern Romance**. Maybe …that's where I got my idea of a perfect love from – those magazines. Anyway, we laughed about how I had to hide the magazines from my parents because they thought that they were too vulgar for me. Maybe they were bad for me; …they made me a dreamer.

'Before we ended our call, I told him that the ninth graders could come to the eighth grade banquet. 'Will you go with me?' I said. Just like that, I invited him to be my guest. After a long silence, maybe five minutes, he said yes. Boy, was I excited – almost too excited. There was a long pause, not because something was wrong with the line but because I didn't know what to say. After I composed myself, for lack of something romantic to whisper, I told him thank you and good night. That was silly but what else could you expect from a 13 year old,

"As soon as I hung up the phone, I called Alice. 'Guess what,' I told her; 'Jack (I called him Jack because Thurston, his first name, sounded too formal, too proper) called me tonight.' I told her that he was going with me to the banquet. She was just as excited as I was and told me that she was going to get a date, too. The next day Alice told me that she was going with Lamar Thomas. A pair of love-struck, giddy girls, we were so happy that we were first time victims of cupid's arrows.

'It's funny that I remember that meeting and those phone calls so clearly. That must have been 54 years ago. Now- a - days, sometimes I can't remember to take my medicine or what day it is. And, believe it or not, for the life of me, I cannot remember how or when I met both my husbands. But, that first meeting, that first phone call, and that first date with Jack stand out in my memory as vividly as the pictures on one of those plasma TVs"

"Tell me about the date?" her granddaughter asked. "It's hard to believe that you had a date that young. You didn't let me date until I was 16."

"Baby, those were different times and children were different; a lot of people married by 14 or 15. Why, my mom and dad married when mom was 14. Anyway," she went on with her story. "I didn't realize it then, but now I know… that date was a harbinger, a kind of warning. But, he had me hooked by then, and I wanted to be caught. My sister Thelma, a teacher at Springville, who was 10 years older than I was, saw the guest list for the banquet. She was excited that I had a date and immediately put plans in action to get me ready for that night".

"What did she do?" Tyriah asked as she settled back in her chair to listen.

"Thelma went to Stephen's Department Store and bought me a sky blue sundress with a cancan underskirt which was just beautiful. She had my hair done at a beauty shop for the first time, and arranged to be our chaperone. Having a chaperone was okay with me. That was the only way my dad would let me go."

"Tell me about the date."

"Well, at the banquet after we had our meal, the tables were moved to the wall of the gym to make room for dancing. Jack moved our table and volunteered to help with the others. That was very polite of him, but he left me at the table with my friend Alice and her date. When the music started and couples drifted on the dance floor, Jack lost himself in the crowd. I sat and sat and sat waiting, but no Jack. Thirty minutes later, I decided to look for him. I found him on the other end of the gym in a circle of boys doing the dog."

"Doing the dog? What was that?"

"Well, let me just say, today's young people dance the twerk. The dog was twice as vulgar as twerking. Those boys paired off, hunched over each other's butts – like dogs – rolling, pushing in and out, howling. The dog was porn masquerading as a dance. Embarrassed is an understatement. When I saw Jack, I was so ashamed that I withdrew to our table and sat there alone and insecure... in that big crowd... the rest of the night. Not much for a first date, was it?"

"Did you date him in high school, grandma?"

"I sure did. In fact, I dated him all through high school. I didn't really have another boyfriend. There was one brief time – about two weeks – when I tried to make Jack jealous."

"What happened?" Tyriah asked laughing and a little surprised that her grandmother was being so opened.

"Well, I heard that Jack had gone to a sock hop with Erma, a pretty girl, popular too."

"A sock hop? What was that, grandma?"

"A sock hop was dance held in the Gym. We danced in our socks to keep from messing up the gym floor. Well anyway, Alice told me that Erma had gone to the dance with Jack. Boy! Was I jealous! So jealous, I guess... I couldn't think straight. I called James, a boy who had been sweet on me for years. And, I pretended to ask about homework. As usually, he asked me for a date before the call was over. I think he was a little surprised that I accepted."

"Where did you go, grandma?"

"Nowhere really. He came over to my house, and we sat in the yard talking. I knew Jack would pass the house coming from football practice, and I wanted him to see us. Sure enough he did".

"Did Jack get jealous? Grandma, you were something!"

"I sure was... I don't know if Jack got jealous or not. He didn't do anything – didn't visit me... didn't call... nothing."

"What did you do then?"

"I got desperate. I called James and asked him to meet me at Ora Mae's (Teenagers gathered there to play records on the jukebox.) , and I got so lovey dove with James in front of everybody there that I gave him my high school ring.

"Did you ever get it back?"

"No I didn't, but I got Jack back. As soon as he heard that James had my ring, He came courting, we made up, and before he left, he gave me his ring. I kept that rings for years and we dated throughout high school."

"Grandma, all those years from junior high to high school... did you and Jack ever 'get busy?'"

"Get busy, ...get busy? Oh, you mean sex. Baby girl, you got some nerves... asking your grand about sex... huh! For your information, no, we didn't get busy, but we came close to it... many times. Every time, though, Jack was gentleman enough to stop. 'Let's wait for marriage, he always told me," continued grandma.

"There was one time that I decided that marriage might not come if I didn't help it along."

"What happened" Tyriah asked laughing as she lend forward making sure not to miss a word.

"Well, it was Jack's graduation night, and I was desperate. I was afraid that if Jack left for college, he's fall in love with one of those college girls and forget about me. I thought that I would give him a little special present for graduation to keep him for myself. You know what I mean. Anyway…"

She mumbled as she gazed straight ahead as if removed from time and space far away from her granddaughter or anyone who knew of her reserved, demure nature. Then, she surprised even herself when she went on….

"We went to his house for a party that his family had planned after his graduation from high school. Lucky for me, we were the first ones there. When he went into his room to change clothes, I followed him, got in his bed, and slowly, very slowly began peeling off my clothes. – The shoes first… then the dress. When I was down to my bra, he joined me in bed, and we kissed long… passionately. I eased my legs around his body, locked them there, and caressed him from head to toe making love with my fingers, my legs; then my whole body melted into his. But, as my hand reached for my panties to shed that last layer hiding my virginity, he stopped me and reminded me of our promised to wait until after marriage. I was unsatisfied, frustrated, and embarrassed… embarrassed that I had offered all of myself only to be pushed aside by a promised… a promised to wait. I put my clothes on as slowly as I had pulled them off; – that time… because I was nervous and unable to see through the tears."

"Lord… Grandma is completely out of it," Tyriah whispered, and then called two times – "Grandma, Grandma!" – shocking her back to reality. When she was sure that her grandmother was herself again, curiosity plodded her until she asked, "Did anyone catch you in Jack's bedroom?"

"No, no one. A few of them teased me saying that I was sad that Jack was leaving for college in two weeks. But, no one suspected. In a way, they were right. I was sad... very sad that I had missed my chance to secure our future together.

"The next day Jack told me that he was sorry about the night before. 'I'll make it worth your wait when we get married after we finish college.' Even a fool could figure that he was talking about five more years."

"Well, did you wait?"

"Really, I waited six more years... four years for Jack to finish college and two years waiting for him after that."

"Why in the world did you wait two years after he finished college? Why didn't you marry when he finished?"

"Vietnam... the Vietnam War stole a lot of young men back then. Two weeks after Jack finished school, he was drafted into the army with immediate deployment. He left so fast... I never got a chance to say good-bye or... a chance to finish what I started on his graduation night. My heart shattered into a thousand pieces, and little did I know; I would never gather those pieces back again.

"Jack's letters came regularly – one every two weeks during his first few months in the service. But, afterward, the letters slowed; sometimes, I got none at all for months.

"Oh, I sent letters, but none came. At first, I spent my nights crying into my pillow and my days looking back... looking back over 12 years of promises. I don't quite remember when... at some point during my looking back, I saw my youth fading. I realized that life was passing me by and if I didn't run and catch it, I'd end up an old maid. I decided to move on..determined not to wait another day.

"One or two months later, I started dating. My first date was a mistake; he was too immature – no future for me at all with him. I soon refused his calls, ignored his advances, and stayed my distance away from him. My second date,

Jared, turned into a whirlwind romance. He was everything that a girl looks for in a man – good looking, good job, and a good car. There was only one thing wrong; he was married with two children but living separated from his wife. I overlooked that little obstacle and dated him anyway. He promised me that he would marry me as soon as he was divorced."

"Was that your first husband?" Tyriah asked interrupting her grandma … trying to hurry her on to end of her story. "Did he keep his promise?"

"Yes, he was my first husband, and he kept his promise alright. On the day that he received his divorce papers, he gave me an engagement ring. When I went to tell my parents the good news, guess what? Jack was there looking for me…: after two years, there he was as if nothing had happened… as if time and space had not come between us."

"What happened?"

"We went to dinner. He had heard about my dating, and instead of blaming me, he apologized for his absence… told me that he was stationed in Germany but was soon deployed to Vietnam…claimed that he was missing in action, and… said he had amnesia for two years. He proposed to me right after we finished our meal."

"What did you do, grandma?"

"I had two proposals in one week, after waiting for Jack more than 12 years; it was hard, but what could I do? I did the honorable thing – told Jack about my engagement. When I told him that I needed time to think, he said that he was leaving for California in two days and gave me 24 hours to make up my mind. Twenty-four hours after two years… didn't seem like much to me. I knew I loved Jack, and Jared was a stand in for me. But, I was different.

"Two years is a long time….A person changes a lot in two years; at least I had. I was not the innocent, virgin girl that Jack had left behind. He was looking for that girl; I thought; … I knew that I could never be that person again. I had not kept my promise. …he sure had not kept his. So, I closed the door on my past with Jack, and a dream of a perfect life with him lingered like smothering ashes in a dying fire,

'I opened a door to a future with Jared who had already begun making good on his promises. I married Jared, my first husband, three months after giving Jack his ring back. To this day… I wonder if I made the right choice… wonder whether a life with Jack would have moved us to a different… better place in our lives… wonder if it would have made a difference with Jack."

"Did you have a good marriage with Jared?"

"Baby, no I didn't. Two weeks into our marriage, Jared's first wife came for her children – took them out of the yard and left without saying a word. Jared followed her and brought them back. From that time on, they tussled over those children, and we fought over him obviously seeing her behind my back. Five years into that marriage, I got pregnant with Jared, Jr. When I needed him most…Jared moved back in with his first wife. I know now… that my marriage was a mistake, one that was destined for failure. I became a habitual daydreamer… always fanaticizing about a happy marriage with Jack but looking for the perfect man"

"Grandma, after you left Jared, did you ever try to get back with Jack."

"He came to see me two year after my divorce; … seven years had passed and life had forced me to distrust the opposite sex. But, my episode with Jared was nothing compared to what Jack had experienced. He had married and divorced twice in that short span of time. His first wife had cheated on him with his best friend. The second wife had taken him for all he had; – the houses, his daughter, all his money, even half of his retirement were gone. Retaliating, he had quit his job as an FBI agent to keep from giving so much of his money to child and spousal support.

"When he asked me to go with him to California to start a new life together, I couldn't make that move. How could I … after a bad marriage with Jared? … How could I trust a man with two ex-wives …a man who had quit his job to keep from supporting his child? I couldn't help thinking that he would do the same to me. … just couldn't make that move. Even though I loved him and those ashes from his love were still burning in my heart and could be easily be fanned alive, I closed the door on Jack a second time and moved on again… looking for the perfect love.

"Jack went on to California without me. Just as he had done before when he left for Vietnam, he called every night, then every week, then every month, and then none at all. He drifted away again. I lost his number… lost all contact with him. And I heard nothing from him for another five years. That was after I married my second husband, your grandfather."

"What happened, grandma?" Tyriah asked wondering if her grandmother could have possibly been telling the truth.

"Jack called and said that he wanted to meet me… said that he needed to talk to me about something very important. I explained that I was married; … 'that might not be a good idea,' I told him. He told me that he was married too… for a third time. And, that it was important … very important that he talk to me. So, I agreed to meet him," she said.

"I managed to get away from your grandfather... told him that I went to a concert. I knew that he could not stand concerts and large crowds, and he would not want to go with me. Really, I didn't lie. I did go to a concert... went all the way to the Superdome in New Orleans. When the concert was over, I went to the airport and waited for Jack there, grandma said.

"I sat in the lobby – seems like forever – afraid that he would not recognize me ... and inwardly wishing that he was coming to rescue me from a second mistake – a loveless married that was not much better that my first. I made up my mind then and there that if he asked me, I would leave with him – leave everything behind – husband, children, job, and all – and start a new life with him at last," her grandmother continued sadly.

"His flight from California was on time."

"Did he recognize you?" Tyriah asked, thinking that her grandmother must have changed a lot since their last meeting.

"Yes, he recognized me... came straight to me; I didn't recognize him until he sat next to me and said hello."

"Why?"

"He was a lady... high heels, dress, weave, lipstick, purse – the works. I recognized his voice, but nothing else. Outwardly, he was completely transformed into a woman. At first, I thought someone was playing a cruel joke on me, but he... or she explained that it was no joke."

"I realized that I've been gay all my life," he told me. "I wanted to tell you in person. I didn't fly down from San Diego as a joke. I am gay. I wanted to tell you after I graduated from college... tried several times, but I couldn't. I enlisted and went to Vietnam instead – l y i n g , running. I know now that my lies have caused many – you and the two women that I married for some – a horrible life. I am sorry and hope you can forgive me."

"I reminded him that he had told me over the phone that he was married. 'I am,' he smiled. 'I am happily married to my soul mate, a man I met while in the service. All those years I was running… running… trying to find myself – not running away from you. I have found myself. I can finally say that I am Jackie, and I am happy. Be happy for me!' he said.

"Oh, my God! My dream of being rescued from a bad marriage… of a happy life with Jack crumbled to the ground like a building, imploded – never to rise again. I sat there speechless… just didn't know what to say. It was hard for me to believe that all those years I had been in love with a … a woman trapped in a man's body. How could anyone be so naïve? How could I have been in love with a… a gay person?" grandma asked, crying.

"When I flashed back, momentarily, over our lives searching for a clue… some hint that Jack was gay, I realized now; there were many. The banquet in junior high, the encounter in his bedroom the night of his graduation from high school, the constant plea to wait until marriage before having sex, the sudden departure for Vietnam after his college graduation: all seemed so clear after that confession. But, why… why didn't I see them before now? I guess I was Fate's fool… pulled like puppets on a string… blinded… destined to a life of yearning for a love that I would never have."

FIVE

Georgia's Date

Mama Georgia was sitting on the porch one autumn evening when she noticed that the sunset was just beautiful. The whole Western sky was a fiery-burnt orange. She had never seen it so bright, so wonderful in the Quarters. And, because it was the beginning of autumn – not too cold and not too hot, harvest time, she called it – the weather was just perfect for her. She could sit on the porch and enjoy the outdoors without the pain of arthritis bothering her. She sat humming "Soon I'll be done with the troubles of the world" as she watched the deer, rabbits, and birds play in the distance.

Like most lonely people, Mama Georgia had a habit of talking to herself. "Georgia," she said, "you better enjoy this sunset and these lovely trees, these flowers, and this good air. The Lord has been good to you. He has allowed you to live 16 years beyond your promised time. He just may be coming for you soon." She paused and then she said, "I better stop this talking to myself. If somebody comes this way and hears me. They'll think I'm crazy." She leaned back in her rocker and laughed, and- like most old people have a tendency to do – in no time she was nodding – then fast asleep.

When she woke, it was dark –blacker than usual. "I'd better get myself inside out of this dark," she said, "before something comes along and gets me. It ain't safe for neither man nor beast out here tonight," she snickered. She moved, pushed herself up by the arms of her rocker, and stood struggling trying to balance herself. When she got her footing, she noticed a little light off to the east. "Now who could that be," she wondered? She turned, hobbled inside, locked, and bolted the door. As if that was not enough, she pulled a chair from the table, leaned it forward and braced it under the doorknob. "It just ain't safe for a widow woman living alone out here these days," she mumbled. "But that will keep him out; whoever that is."

As always, Mama Georgia went through her evening rituals. She prepared her meal. "This time, I think I want something special," she muttered. Smothered pork chops, rice and gravy, candied yams, collard greens, and corn bread were her choices. "Yes, this is a meal fit for a last supper," she said to herself as she sat down to eat. As she clasped her hand together to say a blessing, she looked through her East window and noticed that light again. This time, it was brighter than before. "Looks like a torch light," she said. "I wonder if some hunter is out looking to get a kill tonight. I just hope he doesn't come here."

She finished her blessing, enjoyed her meal, washed and put away the dishes. Then, she decided to retire for the night. "I think I'll get my best gown and use it tonight," she said. "Whoever that is outside hunting just might come this way. You never know. I don't want to be in any old thing if someone comes." So, she chose her new, pale pink, satin gown – the one her husband had given her the Christmas before he died – and she laid it on the bed. "I saved you for something special," she told the gown. "This time is as good as any. You just lay there until I finish my bath."

When she had finished her bath, she put on her gown and went to the mirror to brush her hair. "I'm so old," she said when she saw her reflection staring back at her; "I look just like a corpse in this pale pink gown." She laughed and brushed her hair the same way her mother had taught her to do when she had her first date. "That's good," she said when she finished. "Now I am ready for the night."

"I guess I'll say my prayers first; then I'll checked the windows to make sure they are locked," she said just to remind herself of the last tasks before her sleep. She stood by the side of her bed, bent over slightly, closed her eyes, and prayed: "Oh God, I thank you for a long, prosperous life. Bless the pastor and my church, Lord, and help them to know that I have missed service only because I am not well enough to come. Forgive me for my absence and strengthen my faith here where I am. If I should die before I wake, take me home to glory. In Jesus' name, I pray. Amen."

When she crept to close the East window, Mama Georgia was amazed at how bright that little touch light had become. It glowed so bright that she could see for miles. Why, the whole Eastern sky sparkled as if diamonds –not stars – were sprinkled in it. And, it reminded her of a picture of heaven that she had seen long ago. "Oh, that's the most beautiful light I have ever seen," she sighed. "But, what in the world is going on?"

She turned and saw that the section near her bed was also aglow. Only, the light was more beautiful up close and beckoned her to enter it. "Come into the light; come into the light," she heard as she stood – now fixed in a deadly trance. "Come into the light, Georgia," she heard again. The second time the call came; she recognized the voice of Charley, her husband who had died 15 years before.

"Sweet," Mama Georgia smiled and shook her old body away, "you have come for me at last. I was beginning to think that you had forgotten our date." She walked into that beautiful light, reached and took Charley's hand, and the two ascended a flight of golden stairs disappearing into heaven.

The next morning when the postman came and Mama Georgia was not sitting on the porch waiting for him as usual, he figured that something must be wrong. He knocked on the door but did not get an answer. He tried to open the door, but it was impossible; for it was bolted and jammed with a chair. He walked to the back of the house and peeped through the window of her bedroom. What he saw was a sorrowful sight to him. Mama Georgia was lying, crouched in a fetal position on the floor a few steps from the window – dead. "In that pale pink, satin gown," the postman sighed, "Georgia looks just like a corpse already ready for burial."

SIX

An Arranged Meeting

I am sorry, but I need a few more days off. My mother's problem is more serious than I thought," Jean explained. "I can't possibly leave her now. I hope you understand. I'll have to stay in Daytona a few more days."

"When will you be able to return to work," her boss, Mr. Jackson, asked. "We need you here in New York."

"I know. I know," Jean sighed, "but this time family comes first. I am requesting a family leave of six weeks. If Mother gets better before the six weeks are up, I will be back earlier. But, I can't leave her now. I am all she has. "

Jean ended the call to her boss, and regretted her decision for a while. But, what else could she do? This was her mother – the one who had sacrificed so much so that she could become a lawyer in the first place. She thought about all those days her mother worked two jobs so that she could have the best of everything-even Harvard. And, she remembered, too, how her mother had not complained when it took her a year to get established. She continued to support me even though I was a Harvard graduate with a law degree, thought Jean. "Yes, it's my time now. I know that I have made the right decision. I'll stay home as long as Mother needs me. In fact, she needs me Now."

She walked into the kitchen to see if her mother had finished her breakfast and to see if she needed anything else. To her surprise, her mother was crying and had not touched the food.

"Mom, what's wrong? You don't like your breakfast?" Jean asked trying to guess the reason for the crying.

"That's not my breakfast," she said, "I don't know whose food that is. I want you to take me to have breakfast with Mama. I want to go home."

"Mama? Now Mom, you know that grandmother died five years ago," Jean told her fighting back her own tears. And, even though she tried to keep from crying, Jean could not. It was painful to see her mother so forgetful – so confused. "Lord, help us," she cried as she hugged her mother trying to comfort her. "Come on Mom;" she pleaded. "Eat some of your breakfast." Jean put a spoonful of grits in her mother's mouth, but instead of eating it, she spit it out on her daughter and pushed her away.

"Why didn't you tell me that Mama died?" Her mother shouted. "I bet you didn't even take me to her funeral; did you?" She accused and pushed Jean a second time so hard that she fell back and stumbled several times before she was able to brake the fall. When she corrected herself, Jean did not try to continue the feeding, and she did not argue with her mother. She thought it best to leave her alone for a while. So, she walked out of the kitchen onto porch, sat in the swing, and tried to remember the loving mother who had always been so kind and so smart.

As she sat swinging, Jean remembered scenes – like little snapshots from time, first one and then another with her mother – that she would always cherish. In one, she was a little girl in her mother's classroom at Dayton Elementary. "Oh, how all the students loved her? They just couldn't stop calling my mother's name – Mrs. Ruthie this and Mrs. Ruthie that." She remembered that it made her jealous to see how much attention her mother paid to the other students. "That attention paid off," she sighed, "Mom was named Teacher of the Year that year, and I was so proud of her," she whispered. In another scene, Jean saw herself dressed for prom. And she remembered how her mother had fussed over the dress, made sure that her hair was just right, and wouldn't let her leave until she had taken tons of pictures. She was so full of life then, Jean thought. And Jean relived the pinning ceremony of National Board Certified Teachers. That year, Mom received roses for having a perfect score on the NBCT test, she thought. "She was always so smart, so involved, and so full of life. How had she come to this – a victim of Alzheimer's disease, unable to remember... unable to concentrate... so erratic... so irritable?"

Lost in her thoughts, Jean did not notice her mother when she came onto the porch. However, when Jean looked up, there she was looking as though nothing had happened. And, without saying a word, her mother walked passed her and was walking out of the gate when Jean called to her to come back.

"I am going to walk to Mom. I'll be back in a little bit," her mother hollered to her as she increased her speed and headed out of the gate and into the street. Jean had to rush to get her out of the way of an oncoming car. Luckily, the car swerved and barely missed them both.

"Mom," Jean told her, "You must try hard to remember! Grandmother is dead! You can't go see your mom. Now come back onto the porch." She led her mother back into the house and set a plan in motion to try to keep her from having a fatal accident.

The next day Jean phoned Jefferson's Fence Company and arranged for them to install iron gates with locks. When they were finished, she checked to make sure they were well built – not capable of being opened or broken by her mother or anyone. For extra security, she installed iron bars on all the windows and had them locked, too. With these precautions, her worries that her mother might walk into the street and be killed accidentally were over. She rest assured that she had saved her mother from an untimely death.

No longer afraid that her mother would get out of the house and hurt herself, Jean reconnected with old friends; some she had not seen since high school. One in particular was George, her high school sweet heart. Since he was newly divorced, he was glad she called and pursued her instantly. He was invited over for a movie and some drinks, but he was not satisfied with that. He wanted to take Jean out and reintroduce her to Daytona. He remembered how she loved the races and bought tickets to the 500. When he asked Jean if she wanted to attend, she was reluctant at first because she did not want to leave her mother alone. But, she remembered the security she had installed, remembered how thrilling that race is, and she recanted. "Yes, sure I'll go to the race with you," she said.

On the day of the race, Jean was careful to care for her mother's needs before she left. She helped her with her bath, prepared lunch and watched her eat it, and then made sure she had her medicine. She felt sure that her mother would be safe home alone for a few hours. After all, people with Alzheimer's disease had done it before. "Surely, my mom is no less than all the others," she said as she convinced herself that everything would be all right.

Before George came to take her to the race, Jean double- checked her security plan to assure herself that her mother would be safe. As if that was not enough, she made sure the gate was locked from the outside so that there was no way that her mother could free herself from the inside. With those precautions, Jean was off to the race.

She was gone no more than 30 minutes when her mother got an urge to visit her old home place again. "I want to see Mom again. I told Jean that, days ago," she said. "But, that child just won't listen to me. While she's gone, I'll go by myself." When she was ready to go, she locked the house and went to the gate leading to the street. To her surprise, the gate was locked and she was not able to leave. She tried calling for someone to help her open the gate. But, no one heard her. After a while she gave up trying, went inside, and – typical of Alzheimer's patients – she soon forgot about seeing her mother again.

When four hours had passed and Jean had not returned, her mother became impatient. "I am tired of waiting for Jean," she said. "I am hungry. Jean should have given me supper by now. If you want something done, sometimes you have to do it yourself," she complained. With that thought, she decided to cook a meal of fried chicken herself. She seasoned the chicken and put the cooking oil on the stove to heat. But before she could put the chicken in the frying pan, she got an urge to use the bathroom.

In the bathroom, she picked up her puzzle book to work as she relieved herself. The puzzle she selected was a teaser, and she became engrossed in it. She soon forgot the chicken and the oil on the stove and went from the bathroom to her bedroom to sit in her rocker and finish her puzzle. As she often did, she fell asleep. In her slumber, she did not notice the smell of smoke, nor did she hear the cracking sound as the fire engulfed the kitchen, and then the rest of the house. The neighbors tried to get in to save her, but the locked iron gates and the barred windows prevented them from getting to her soon enough. Sadly, Jean's mother never woke, she never heard the sirens or commotion outside; for she was too weak from inhaling the smoke, and she died there in her sleep before she was rescued....

At the funeral, the pastor briefly stopped his sermon and spoke directly to Jean. He commended her for putting her career on hold for her mother and told her that she should not feel guilty that she was not there when her mother died. "You have been a good daughter," he guaranteed her, "but you could not keep death away even if you were there. Death," he said, "is an appointment that we cannot cancel – no matter how hard we try. When our time comes, neither an iron gate nor a barred window will keep him away. It was not just ironic," he continued, "that the precautions you took to save your mother were the very things that aided her death. It was God's plan to arrange a meeting for her with her mother again."

SEVEN

Head Noises

It started about three days ago," sighed Shelley as she turned her head from side to side trying to stop the noise.

"What does it sound like?" asked Dr. Jones reaching for his otoscope.

"It's a low screeching noise that goes on continuously. Could it be something in my ear?" Shelley asked pulling on her ear lobe hoping a tug might give a little relief.

Dr. Jones put his otoscope into the ear canal and examined Shelley's ear closely. "That looks good," he said. "I don't see any ear wax buildup, and there isn't a hole in the ear drum. As far as I can tell from this point, there is nothing wrong with your ear. However, I can order some tests to get a better picture. I am going to schedule a hearing test for next Wednesday to see if you have a hearing loss that might be causing the noise. We will do the test in this office here on Louisiana Avenue. Be here for 9 a.m. If you do not keep the appointment, be sure to notify us at least 24 hours ahead of time."

"Don't worry," said Shelley, "I will definitely be here. I don't think that I can go on much longer. This noise is driving me crazy."

On Wednesday morning, Shelley arrived early for her appointment, and after a twenty-minutes wait, she was ushered into the examining room. "Put on these earphones. I am going to play some tones," the examiner said. "Tell me if you can hear these sounds." One after another, Shelley responded to a faint, a then low, a muffled, and then a high-pitched sound. As if to confuse her, the examiner replayed the tones mixing them. However, each time, Shelley was able to give a correct response. "We are about half finished, said the examiner. However, I need to do the same for the right ear." When the examiner had finished both ears and the test was over, he could only determine that Shelley had a slight hearing loss.

"You have a slight hearing loss, but not enough to cause concern or to order hearing aids," Dr. Jones said, as he explained the results to Shelley. "There is one more test that I can order that will rule out whether there is anything wrong with your inner ear. I am going to schedule an MRI to see if you have a tumor, some stroke damage, or some... abnormality. I need you to report to North Shore MRI on Friday morning at 9 a.m."

As scheduled, Shelley took the long, 30-minutes test and waited to hear the results during her next appointment. However, before her next appointment, the noise in her ear changed from that faint screeching sound to a loud irritating clicking noise, much like the sound that a hundred cicadas might make singing in chorus on a warm summer day. It was nerve-wracking, mainly because it would not let up. "Something must be done," Shelley said to herself in desperation. "I can't sleep; I can't get any relief." She tried eardrops and poured hot oil in her ear to no avail. The noise clicked on, and on, and on, non-stop. As a result, she was a bundle of nerves. "I can't go on! I can't go on this way!" She cried.

The night before her appointment, Shelley turned her head to the right to look at her cat playing in the corner. To her surprise, a new sound joined the constant clicking. She heard a distinct shake, shake sound – like maracas music. She turned her head again to see if the noise would sound again. It did. In fact, all that night she tossed and turned unable to get any sleep or get a break from the shake, shake, click, clicking in her head. She thought that something was indeed wrong and could hardly wait to see the doctor the next day. "Surely, he will give me something to relieve the noise," she said.

"Well," Mrs. Shelley, said the doctor as he gave the results of the MRI. "I am glad to report that you don't have a tumor or any damage in the inner ear. The sound you hear is most likely tinnitus."

"What can you do to help me," asked Shelley hopefully?

"Well, there is really nothing that I can do."

"Nothing! You can't prescribe anything?"

"No, but you can try to mask the noise at night by listening to white noise. There is a machine at Walmart that might help you get some rest at night."

Shelley left the doctor's office discouraged. He had told her good news; after all, she did not have a tumor. However, he had done absolutely nothing to help her nerve-wracking problem. The noise was still there –maybe forever – shake, shake, shaking, click, click, clicking in her head.

Outside the doctor's office, Shelley phoned her mother and asked if she could meet her for lunch. "Sure, I need some time away from this house," her mother said.

"Good," "I'll meet you at Piccadilly at 11." Ending the call, Shelley wondered how her mother would react to the news of her noise. *I certainly hope that she doesn't think I am crazy. How in the world am I going to tell her.*

By the time her mother arrived, Shelley was a bundle of nerves, and she broached the problem as soon as her mother sat down.

"Mom," Shelley paused then continued, "I am having a problem."

"What kind of problem? You look as though you haven't slept in days."

"Promise me you won't laugh...I hear noises; I hear noises, she repeated.

"Noises?"

"Yes, noises. I've been seeing an ENT, but he told me today that there is nothing that he could do. I don't think I can go on like this. The noise just won't stop; it just goes on, and on, and on constantly." Then she leaned over near her mother and whispered, "Can't you hear it?" Her mother listened, but she could not hear anything. However, she did notice how nervously Shelley's right leg was shaking and how erratic her behavior had become. She also sensed that her daughter was losing control.

"You need a second opinion," her mother said worriedly. "Why don't you see a neurologist? He may be able to help."

Shelley took her mother's advice and arranged through her primary care doctor to see a neurologist. He was very thorough. Starting with a physical exam, he ordered a CAT scan and an MRI, but the results were again disheartening.

He could not find anything physically wrong with her either, and he suggested that Shelley was having a break down. When he told her that he was going to refer her to a psychiatrist, Shelley lost it. "A psychiatrist," she shouted. "I am not crazy! I hear noises! I hear noises; I tell you, and they are getting louder and louder!" She cried. "I don't see why you can't hear them, too. Can't you hear them? Can't you hear them? They are certainly loud enough!"

The doctor offered to give her a sedative, but Shelley refused. Because he had not given a solution, she left that office worse than before. Her nerves were visibly on edge. The least bit of noise outside of her head made her jump, and the noise inside her head drove her insane. "The nerve of him suggesting that I am crazy! He's the one crazy, if he thinks I am going to pay that bill." Shelley laughed as she narrowly missed a car because she ran a red light. "Watch out!" She yelled at the other car. "What do you think red lights are for?"

During the next few days, Shelley slowly slipped into depression. Her daily duties became overwhelming, and the house was a mess. She couldn't eat, couldn't sleep, and couldn't concentrate on anything but the noise. "Stop! Stop!" At last, she cried as if the noise could obey her command. "Stop it now!" When the noise would not stop, she turned the TV on and its volume up hoping to drown the noise. However like everything else, it did not work. "White noise," she said, "the doctor said get some white noise." So, she plugged in her noise machine, and like a cruel joke, the effects took a sinister turn for the worst. The noise in her head drowned out the white noise and became a whisper that sang to her, "Kill it! Kill it! Kill it!"

Shelley took her gun from the drawer of the bedside table– with no intention of hurting herself. For, she only wanted to kill the noise – to force it into the background. "That noise machine would not work. I bet this will," she cried, as she shot into the roof of her room. Boom! The gun was loud, but not loud enough to mask the noise. Instead of fading, the click, clicking and shake, shaking join chorus with the sinister whispering and the noise became unbearable – haunting her, harassing her, challenging her.

"Kill it! Kill it! Kill it!" Shelley heard the whispering above the click, clicking and shake shaking. In desperation…in her deepest despair… in her darkest depression, she put the gun to her left ear –   the one with the most noise. "White noise would not stop you," she sneered; "and the gunshot would not kill you. I bet this will! Take this," she mocked. Boom! Boom!

She fell a few feet away from the TV and lay there drifting into nothingness. The last words that she heard were those of Dr. Travis: "Stay tune for a miraculous cure for head noises," he said, as **The Doctors**, broke for a commercial.

EIGHT

Sometimes I Look at Sinners

Greenville, a small village in Southeast Mississippi, was far enough away from everywhere to escape the hustle and bustle of life in the city with its murders, its jammed traffic, its homelessness, its street beggars, its graffiti, and its filth. However, it was close enough to allow its citizens the opportunity to travel within an hour's drive to a number of towns for shopping, for medical attention, for employment, or for entertainment. The largest towns near it were New Orleans about 65 miles to the south and Mc-Comb, Mississippi about 40 miles to the west. The people in Greenville traveled to those towns only when necessary, for they preferred the quietness and the peace of life in the country.

There were no more than about 250 families living in Greenville years ago. The whole incorporated area of its village consisted of a Piggy Wiggly grocery store, a US Post Office, a Chevron gas station, and believe it or not, a café,

The Catfish House. Two public schools, Greenville High for whites and Booker T. Washington High for blacks, were focus points in the out skirts of the village. For employment, the people worked at the schools, traveled 12 miles to do shift work at Riverside Paper Mill in nearby Franklin, found work in New Orleans, or engaged in truck farming to get by.

Nothing much ever happened in Greenville except that one time when there a massacre of blacks by the Klan, but that was long ago, so long that no one remembers it – not even the history books. For years the Klan terrorized with their burning crosses, their KKK signs mysteriously appearing on roads, buildings, and black churches. But that too was long ago – more than 50 years. White- only signs disappeared in the late 1960s; the public schools integrated in the mid-1970s without needing the National Guard or US troops like in some Southern towns back then. By the 1980s, signs of segregation had all disappeared within a 50- miles radius of Greenville. And, the fear of the Klan surfaced only once for a brief time when David Duke, a white- supremacist and former Grand Wizard of the KKK, ran for governor of nearby Louisiana, but it died shortly after he disappeared from Mandeville. So... for more than 20 years blacks and whites in Greenville and nearby Riverside enjoyed a relationship free from racial disharmony.

The peace and quietness, the location away from the big city, the void of racial disputes, and the lure of public schools needing teachers: these are the reasons Mallory Smith considered Greenville when she was trying to find a job just out of college in the early 1980s. It was the perfect place for her. For, she was a country girl at heart. Her teen years were spent working from sun up to sun down in her father's cotton field. She had been no more than 45 miles away from home and had known nothing about city life. Though she had read about places like Paris and had seen the snow- capped mountains of Kilimanjaro and the Niagara River with its beautiful water falls in books, she had no desire to go to those places. "Just give me the country; that's the life for me," she would laugh and say mimicking a line from her favorite show, **Green Acres**.

Mallory's mother had protected her from life's ills- no drinking, no late- night parties, no wild friends, and no mini-skirts showing much too much. She was naive when she left home back then, and she was still naïve over 30 years later.

Mallory hurried out of school trying to beat the afternoon rush of students leaving the campus. She noticed that her gas was low and pulled into Chevron to refuel. When she got out of her car she saw Skeeter, a student that she had not seen for a while.

"Hi Skeeter, how are you?" Mallory asked with a smile as she began pumping gas.

"I'm okay Mrs. Mallory. Is school out yit?"

"Yes."

Sloppy drunk, Skeeter stumbled toward his car, stood, turned, and staggered back clumsily toward Mallory. "Mrs. Mallory," he said, "can I speak to ya a minute?"

"Sure. I always have time for my favorite student. What is it?"

"Mrs. Mallory, I jist want ya to know that I didn't have nothing to do wit what dem redneck's doin'. You know it's a shame, and dey did it in the church, too."

"What are you talking about Skeeter? Who did what?"

"My church… and dey call deyselves Christians. I can't tell you what dey did, or I'd be in trouble, too. I jist want ya to know that I didn't have nothing to do with it. I ain't got nothing 'gainst blacks. Dey even made out a list."

"What kind of list," Mallory asked.

Skeeter did not answer, but he awkwardly hugged his former teacher longer than he had ever done before. Even though she smelled cheap whiskey on his breath, and his clothes were filthy, Mallory hugged him back. My God, she thought, Skeeter is drunker than an Irishman on St. Patrick's Day. As he walked unsteadily away, she wondered, how in the world can I take him seriously? And, when he was pulling away, she shouted to him, "Be careful!"

Driving away from the Chevron, Mallory remembered that Thomas "Skeeter" Jones was drunk the last time she saw him. It had been years since he was in her class insisting to be called "Skeeter" each time she called him Thomas – That was 1979, three years after the black and the white schools consolidated in Forrest County. Skeeter had taken her English II class for two years and had not passed it. On his third try to pass English II, he enrolled in Mrs. Hadley's class, hoping that if he took the class under a white teacher, he would pass it. Unfortunately, he had failed that one too. He later told Mallory that he realized that he was not cut out for school and that he was dropping out in the spring.

At first, Skeeter's words gnawed at Mallory as a puzzle or a problem would challenge an inquisitive student. Just what did he mean; she worried all the way home. Doing her evening chores, she tried to piece a puzzle together. "Was he talking about my former students doing something to hurt me? No, that couldn't be it. Those children seemed to adore me." During supper Mallory mentioned the conversation to her husband, Dave.

"Do you mean the Skeeter you talked so much about right after the school merged," he said with a grin as he cut his pork chop in little squares. "If I were you, I wouldn't worry about it. Didn't you say he said that he was not cut out for school? Even Skeeter realizes that he is not all there. Forget about it."

Later that night Mallory settled down to her usual before bedtime ritual of grading essays. As always, her students' work captured her attention. This paper is so disorganized and full of simple mistakes, she thought as she frowned at John's, her weakest student's paper. How can I give him constructive criticism without killing his desire to write? As she considered what she would write on John's comment sheet, her chance meeting with Skeeter drifted to the back of her mind and slowly faded away like rings of ripples undulating in disturbed water. When she eased in bed beside her sleeping husband, she had completely forgotten about Skeeter and his so-called rednecks.

The next morning as soon as Mallory opened the classroom door and entered her room, the intercom blared, "Mrs. Mallory, I need to see you in the office. Come here before you go to your duty post."

"Yes. I sure will," Mallory called back as she set her books on her desk. Taking a note pad and pen for just- in-case, she hurried to the office, wondering what Mr. William could possibly want that early.

"Have a seat, Mr. William, the principal, said, as he pointed to a chair in front of his desk. "It sure is cold today for an October day," he added. He did not like small talk, but he struggled to find some way to tell Mallory the bad news about a non renewal letter that the superintendent had given him to give to her that day. So, to ease into this uncomfortable subject, he asked about her son, about her classes, and even about her dog, and then he thought that he needed to finish this ungodly task so she could go to her duty post before the bell sounded.

Without so much as a hint of sympathy, Mr. William said in the most scornful tone, "Mrs. Mallory, I have a letter here for you from Superintendent Jones. Oh, by the way, I need you to sign for it."

'What is it? I hope it's not one of those non renewal letters," Mallory said jokingly but secretly hoping that it was not. 'I heard Greenville's non certified teachers got theirs yesterday."

"You guessed it. That's exactly what it is," he told her.

"You must be kidding me," she laughed. Then, realizing that he was not joking, she reasoned, "I am a certified teacher. I have done everything I was supposed to. My teaching certificate is up-to-date, my lesson plans are always on time, and my student's scores have the greatest improvement in the school. Plus, I just passed the National Board. I know dammed well you are joking, Why would I get a non renewal letter?"

"I don't know," he said nervously. " Mr. Jones said that you have five days in which to request a hearing. Otherwise, your dismissal is final."

'This must be a mistake," Mallory said trying to convince him that it indeed was a mistake.

"You can arrange a conference with the superintendent," he said as he pushed an affidavit toward the front of the desk for Mrs. Mallory to sign.

The 7:30 a.m. bell sounded before Mallory had a chance to reach her before-school duty post. At the bell, she turned and walked, as if in a trance, slowly toward her classroom. It was amazing how quickly her joking had turned into worry. The pink letter in her hand made sure of that. Why did she get a letter? What was she going to do without a job? How would she pay the bills? Who could she turn to for help? She considered calling MAE, her Association of Educators, but remembered that it might be best to talk to the superintendent first. She decided to call him during her 9 o'clock break. Then her eyes focused on the letter in her hand and she thought to hide it from the students and her coworkers. She slipped it inside her sweater and held it under her arm. She heard but did respond when a student yelled, "You are on the wrong side of the hall, Mrs. Mallory. And you are always telling us to walk on the right side. Don't you see you are bumping into people?"

Mallory reached her door at the same time as the first student. How am I going to get through the day, she thought as she flashed a forced smile and said, "Good morning. It's a lovely day!" –When the last student came in, she closed her door and walked carefully to her desk. "My God," she whispered, "It would be a disaster if I dropped the letter in front of this class." She bent down, pulled out the bottom desk drawer, and pushed the letter under a stack of graded papers. When she began calling her roll, a student reminded her that she had forgotten to give a bell ringer. "Oh yes, the bell ringer," she said as she reached for the stack of "Bell Ringer Number 69," labeled Vocabulary. She gave the stack to a student, instructing her to pass them out. Then she got her roll book and silently began to check it. "Have any of you seen Larry this morning?" She questioned.

"Mrs. Mallory, he's right there on the second row in front of you. What's wrong with you?" A student said jokingly.

"What's wrong with me? There's nothing wrong with me," she said. "The question is, why are you taking so long to finish that bell ringer? A bell ringer is just a five minutes exercise meant to give me time for roll call and lunch check. Pass your papers in now," she yelled!

When some students begged for more time, and others complained that she was being a little pushy, Mallory realized that something was indeed wrong. She could not take her mind off the letter and her impending clash with Superintendent Jones. That worry was causing her to make some simple mistakes. It was not like her to walk on the wrong side of the hall, to miss a student sitting right in front of her, or to yell at her students. "How am I going to get through the day?" She whispered so loudly that she was afraid that the students in front heard her. Her worry turned into nervousness when she looked at the clock and saw that it was only 8 o'clock. The day was just beginning.

During morning break after the last student left the room, Mallory locked her door and took her cell phone out of her brief case. She phoned the school board office. "You have reached Forrest County Schools. This is the superintendent's office. May I help you?" she heard the secretary's high-pitch voice say.

"May I speak with Mr. Jones, please?"

"I'm sorry, he's not in today."

"When do you expect him back?"

"Mr. Jones is out of town. He is not expected back until the Monday after break."

"Monday," Mallory repeated as she hung up the phone and placed it back into her briefcase. "Monday, I have to wait until after the fall break to speak to Mr. Jones. That means that my five days to responds to will be gone by then. I can't do this... I can't do this!" She pulled the call box string and told the school secretary that she needed to take off rest of the day.

The 14 miles ride home seemed longer than usual. On most days she used her driving time to unwind and for a few minutes forgot the stress caused by the bureaucracy of state laws, by the disrespect of unconcerned, rowdy students, and by the lack of necessary paper, pens, books, or computers to make her job easy. All she had to do, once she got in her car, was to turn on her music and play a spiritual or some blues. Either would do to take away her cares and to reassure her that teaching was worth it. When she felt a low throbbing headache radiating on both sides of her temple, she played her favorite song, "Turn Back the Hands of Time" by Tyrone Davis. She thought that that was all she needed to do to sooth the pain. But her music did not work. Even though she hummed the words, her mind betrayed her and drifted back on the events of the morning. How could he do that? She wondered. What if I cannot get an appointment with him before my five days are up? "How could he pass out a pink slip and leave town without giving me a chance to find out why," she screamed out loud as tears rolled downs her cheeks.

By the time she pulled into her driveway, her eyes were red from crying, her headache was an excruciating migraine, and her nerves were on edge, twitching like dull needles sticking from under her skin. –She sat in the car collecting her thoughts, considering her next move, and giving her red eyes time to clear before she made an attempt to go in inside. When she opened her car door something stole her attention. A small, black worker ant was crawling along, dragging the larvae of a butterfly. It was a heavy load for such a small creature. It came in full view when she stepped on the pavement. On an impulse, she thought, kill it! She lifted her foot and came down on the ant with a stomp hard enough to kill a much larger insect. "Why did I do that?" She whispered.

As she fell back on her car seat, her mind raced out –of-control from one thought to another. "All pieces of the entire world" she considered, "are schemed so that even the most minute piece like that ant, work together to enhance the whole. Sometimes a small life form feeds on a larger one; only to become the feast of one greater than itself. But I had no intentions of eating that ant or using it for my benefit. Why did I crush it?" she whispered. "Life is like a giant puzzle, her mind raced again; each piece fits just so to complete a beautiful picture. The question is: what piece am I? If I am crushed like that ant for no reason at all will my absence upset the whole order of God's plan?"

At that thought Mallory struggled to pull her together, to get her mind under control so that she could spend her time thinking about more important things, like how she was going to save her job. The thought of her job reminded her that she had left the letter in her desk drawer at the school. "Oh my God! What if the sub sees it," she cried out. She quickly closed her car door and backed out of her driveway into the path of a tractor-trailer. She pulled on the side of the road just in time to escape a foreseeable- fatal accident. I must be careful, she thought as she rushed more than 75 miles an hour back to school to get that letter. When she got there, she drove around to the back, entered the door near her classroom, and observed that her wing was still out to lunch. She unlocked her door – and unnoticed, got the letter and left the school as hurriedly as possible…. Thank God, the principal had not seen her.

When Mrs. Mallory returned to her house the second time, she did not linger outside. Instead, she went quickly into her office and searched for the phone number of her MAE representative. She did not find it easily. It was not in either of her desk drawers, and it was not in the file cabinet. When she reached for her briefcase to see if she had one in there, her son, Tony, called out as he walked downstairs from his room, "Mom, is that you! What are doing home so early?"

"I had some problems at school today. I'll tell you about them in a little while."

"I need to tell you something too, he said as he leaned against the door to her office."

"I don't have time right now, Tony: I need to call MAE before the representative leave for the day."

"But Mom," he said, "it's important. Those people won't leave me alone."

What could be more important than trying to save my job, she thought as she looked at her son – trying to hide her worry.

"I need to talk to you," he said again, this time with his head hung low and tears dripping from his eyes as he dragged himself back to his room. "I need to talk to you, Mom."

Mallory called out to him, "I'll come to your room as soon as I finish this." She phoned MAE and was surprised when the rep answered. "May I speak to someone about a non renewal letter," she said.

"I'll connect you to Lawyer Sinclair; hold a minute." Click....

When the lawyer answered, Mallory explained that the principal had given her a non renewal letter, that the superintendent was out- of- town for the week, and that she needed advice. "Well first," he said, "You have five days in which to request a hearing."

"How can I do that when he's nowhere to be found?"

"Get some paper and take this down." Sinclair told her to request a hearing in a certified letter addressed to the superintendent. "Once the secretary signs for the letter, the superintendent must give you a hearing," he explained. He cautioned her to act quickly and to be sure to send the letter certified so that she can have proof that she acted within the time frame. "Did the letter give the reason for your dismissal?" he questioned.

"Yes," she told him. "It said budgetary reasons."

"Well then, ask the superintendent to provide proof to support budget problems. Tell him you need to see a certified copy of the budget showing total income from all sources, expenses, disbursements and balances. Also, indicate that you will have a legal representative present at the hearing. Don't worry," he assured her; "everything will be okay."

Hanging up the phone, Mrs. Mallory wondered what her son could possibly want to talk to her about. She took a deep breath and composed herself before she left her office. She did not want her son to worry about her; so she decided not to talk to him about her problem. After all, she had done a lot of that lately – not talk to him. She was always too busy with work, with other children, with house chores… to talk to him. Most times, she spent so much time with students' problems that she had no time for her own child. This time, after 20 or 30 minutes, she decided to see what he wanted, and she climbed the stairs leading to the bedrooms.

Near his room, she noticed that her son's door was slightly open. She knocked but did not get an answer; she knocked again. The door opened completely and revealed a shocking scene, a limp body lying in a fetal position with vomit draining from the corner of his mouth. There was an empty bottle of sleeping pills and an empty bottle of her pain pills on the bedside table. Scattered on the floor were several of both kinds of pills, as if they had accidentally fallen while so many were being stuffed in his mouth. A spent bottle of 96 proofs Jack Daniels was clutched in his right- hand and crumpled in his left- hand was a note. A nervous wreck, she rushed to the phone and called 9-1-1.

"I need an ambulance at 902 Highway 210 quickly! My son has taken what looks like an overdose. Get somebody here quickly, please!" Mallory hung the phone up, pried the note from her son, and read in disbelief, "I can't go on like this. They won't leave me alone. I am better off dead."

"Oh my God!" she cried hysterically, "Tony, what have you done? Tony, Tony, what have you done?!!" She felt his pulse. It was faint, but he was alive.

At Mercy Hospital in nearby Riverside, Tony was rushed into ICU, and. Mallory was not allowed to enter. She sat nervously in the waiting room crying; wondering what could possibly have gone wrong. What could make a level- headed

17- year -old try to kill himself she wondered? Then she remembered the note: "I can't go on like this. They won't leave me alone." It didn't make sense to her. Who were they? What were they doing to him?

Unable to come up with an answer, she walked over to the window and looked at the parking lot near the ER. Dave should have gotten here by now, she thought as she surveyed the cars below looking for him. "Where in the world is he? I called him right after I finished talking to 911. He should be here by now," she whispered as went back to her seat. "Why am I so worried?" She reasoned. "Students overdose all the time and are back in school within two weeks. As soon as the doctor finishes pumping his stomach, Tony is going to have to answer to me – the idea of him putting us through all this trouble."

At that thought, she saw the doctor and a nurse approaching her, and she sensed that something was not right.

"How is he? Is everything alright?" She hesitantly asked.

Shaking his head, the doctor told her, "No… we were unable to save him. I am sorry!" He said as he reached to console her.

"What do you mean? You were unable to save him?"

"He stopped breathing; … we tried, but we could not resuscitate."

"Could not resusci…," she stammered as she fainted and dropped to the floor.

Lifting her into a chair, the doctor shouted to an aide in the hallway to get some cold water. By the time the aide returned though, Mallory had come to herself, but she was crying hysterically.

"Lord, I have killed my son….I have killed Tony," she cried, as she rocked back and forth.

When Dave arrived, saw the doctor, nurses, and curious on-lookers surrounding his wife, saw the pain and horror etched on her face like that of Caravaggio's **Medusa**, he could not believe how frantically unnerved she was. "What on earth is going on?" He pleaded trying to make sense of it all. "Why are you here?" He asked moving close to comfort her. "Nothing can be so terribly bad," he told her as he rubbed her back and then her neck trying to calm her.

"It's Tony."

"What about Tony?"

"He's gone," she cried. "I've killed our son"

"What do you mean?" Dave asked. He knew what she meant, but he could not utter the word killed and could not conceive that anything so drastic had happened to his family. "Not Tony, not Tony," he stammered. "You didn't!"

"Yes," she cried, rocking back and forth, "Tony, our Tony is dead. And it's my fault! It's my fault!"

The nurse interrupted Dave and his wife and explained to him that Tony was brought into emergency with an overdose of pain pills, and that they had tried but could not save him. She assured him that his wife was completely innocent of their son's death.

"Yes," the doctor said, "your son's death was his fault and his only." The doctor expressed his sympathy, told the nurse to complete the necessary papers and excused himself.

"Let's move into my office," the nurse said to the Davises as she pointed to a small office within the ER room. Once there and out of the prying eyes of onlookers, she expressed sympathy but went straight to the business at hand. "Will you give us permission to harvest Tony's organs; the nurse asked addressing both parents? There is a great need for organs of all kinds and your son will live on in so many people if you do."

The Davises sat stunned but considered the possibility that their son could live on. They both visualized their child happy and healthy – smiling with his friends. His smiling made it impossible for either to say yes. For, they could not imagine their son anywhere – on earth or in heaven – without his organs. "No, we can't do that," they both whispered.

"Will you give me consent to use Tony's body for research?" The nurse asked. "Universities have a great need for cadavers. Giving such a donation will do much to advance medical study."

"…Medical study! Lady, please! No, you may not cut his body in any way for study," Dave yelled squirming and annoyed. When the nurse noticed how upset she was making Dave, she withdrew and asked to what funeral home should we send the body?

"If you don't mind, I will send him to the Heavenly Gates, the white funeral home on Jefferson Davis Avenue; they have started taking black people and they provide a very good service," she said.

"No," Mrs. Mallory told her. "Our family uses Crain on Sullivan Drive; send him there." After they signed the necessary papers, Dave and Mallory left for home. Once outside the hospital, she asked, "Didn't it seem strange that the nurse wanted to send Tony to Heavenly Gates?"

"Yes, and she sure was trying to get Tony's body, too. – A bit pushy, I'd say," Dave said, still upset over the thought of using Tony for medical research. "The nerves of her!"

Home the next day, searching through Tony's things, trying to find answers, Dave asked his wife, "Why did you say that you killed Tony when we were at the hospital?"

"He tried to talk to me," she explained, "a little before I found him unconscious, but I was too busy for him. I was too wrapped up in myself. I was trying to check on a letter that the principal had given me this morning. When I finally went to his room to talk to him, it was too late. The note said that he couldn't go on like this. He was talking about me... he was talking about me." She cried anew when guilt consumed her as fire consumes a wooden building. And, she struggled because of the burning pain and agony of it. "Lord, have mercy, have mercy on me," She moaned.

In an effort to comfort her, Dave hugged her to him and whispered, "That's a silly idea. Get rid of it! It's not your fault; ... it's not your fault." Though he tried to comfort her, she could not escape the burning pain.

Planning Tony's funeral proved impossible for Mallory. She could not stand the idea of having to plan a funeral and not a graduation party or a wedding for her son. The very thought of a funeral for a child – her child – made her sicker with grief, and too quickly, her burning guilt slipped into a chasm of depression. She tried to hide her depression from Dave with a disguise of strength, but the force of it was too much to bear. When they went to arrange the funeral for Tony, tears betrayed her, and her sham was uncovered. Standing before a casket, she trembled and fell to her knees. "Oh, Lord," she cried, "Give me strength!" When Dave moved to help her up, she yelled to him, "You are going to have to do this alone! I can't do it... I can't do it!"

So Dave, who had always been passive in handling family business and in making personal decisions for the family, stepped up to be the pillar that Mrs. Mallory needed so much to lean on. He finished the arrangements – plot, flowers, casket, programs, repast, wake, all were in place. And the funeral was set for the next Saturday. In between time, he received the well-wishers – who came bringing food and offering aid – and made excuses for his wife who was, by then, so sick with grief that she was too incoherent to carry on a decent conversation. To the onlookers, he appeared a mountain of strength, and a neighbor told him, "It's a blessing that the Lord has allowed you to stand strong at such a grievous time in your life." Little did they know that when Dave was out of the sight of all, especially his wife, he too was a nervous wreck. For them, he was merely a mirage.

On Friday when Dave went to preview the body to approve it – to make sure that their son's hair, clothes, and appearance was just right – before the undertaker displayed it for the wake, he had to force himself to stand beside the casket and look down on it. As he did, all his emotions – the grief for his son, the fear for his wife's health, the feeling of guilt for his son's death, and the hate for a God who had allowed such tragedy – swelled in him and overflowed from his eyes. He could no longer pretend to be that solid rock that his wife needed. . . And like her he trembled and crumbled to his knees –crying, moaning like a child. But unlike her, he grabbed his chest, felt the squeezing pain, and struggled for his breath before he passed out.

The secretary rushed to phone 9-1-1, the undertaker administered CPR , and an ambulance was dispatched to the funeral home. Within minutes, Dave was on his way to Mercy Hospital. Before he arrived though, the paramedic checked his vital signs, recorded his symptoms, and gave him aspirins.

"Chew these aspirins then hold them under your tongue," the paramedic told him as they turned into the ER's entrance. "They should ease the effects of that heart attack."

Dave could not speak, but he frowned and raised his brow as if to ask, did I have a heart attack?

"You sure did, Mr. Davis," the paramedic answered sensing Dave's thought from his expression. "You sure did."

"I think I'll take a nap and settle my nerves before Dave returns. I don't want to look too bad at the wake tonight. – Maybe a nap will help," Mallory. said as she settled in her recliner and tried to drift off. Unfortunately, she found it was impossible. Instead of sleeping, she lay there with her mind busy – racing... replaying little scenes from week. The picture of Tony lying in a fetal position with the crumpled note in hand, the empty whiskey bottle in the other, and the pills scattered on the floor, flicked by more than once. She also saw the doctor and nurse coming out the ER looking sinister and distorted with the news of Tony's death. Then she saw a scene that had been forced into the background. It was of Mr. William, her principal handing her the pink slip. "Oh, my God," she cried, "I've been so worried about Tony that I completely forgot my job... I forgot to tell Dave about the letter. Lord, I have lost my job!". Just then, the phone rang and she stopped her reruns to answer it. "Hello"

"This is the ER receptionist at Mercy Hospital in Riverside. I am calling to inform you that your husband was admitted to our ER a while ago. We need you here as soon as possible."

"Oh my God, what could possibly be wrong... now!" Mrs. Mallory sighed as she hung up the phone and searched for her keys. 'Dave was just fine when he left for the funeral home. What could have gone wrong? Oh, he's okay," she assured herself. 'I'm just a worrywart!" And, she did not rush through the traffic.

When she arrived, walked into the ER, and saw several patients with heart monitors and breathing machines hooked to them, Mallory felt the gravity of her being summoned there. And she suddenly became concerned... then nervously worried about her husband as she walked into the nurse's office.

"Mrs. Mallory?" The nurse asked looking up from a stack of papers on her desk. "I've been waiting for you. Have a seat."

Mallory, eased into the chair in front of the desk, tried to composed herself, and hesitantly asked, "What is it?"

"Your husband... he had a heart attack... well he had two heart attacks. The paramedics were able to stabilize him for the first one. But we were unable to save him during the second. ...He passed away an hour ago. I'm so sorry!"

"You must be mistaken. My husband was fine this morning. You must be mistaken," Mrs. Mallory repeatedly refused to believe that such misfortune could happen to her... to her family. "Where is he...? Where is Dave?" She asked almost dazed.

The nurse led her to a small cubicle in the back of the ER, pulled back the curtain shielding a bed there, and sure enough Dave lay lifeless with his eyes wide open. He had been disconnected from all life support but nothing else. He was still wearing the clothes that he had worn to the funeral home that morning. And, if it were not for his eyes, – staring with that frantic gaze as if he had been frightened unto death – he would have appeared asleep.

The sight of her husband's corpse ripped her heart in two as Mallory stood looking down on him, and the rest of her body turned to stone. She felt nothing. No pain... no discomfort... no guilt... no sorrow – nothing. It was as if she too had died.

"Mrs. Mallory, can I get you anything? Let me get you a cup of coffee," the nurse asked.

"No, I'm okay."

"Well, let's go back into my office where you can sit down."

In the office again, the nurse went through her routine for releasing a body. She had Mrs. Mallory sign the necessary relief forms to send the body for an autopsy and then to the funeral home – Crain on Sullivan Drive. But, before she could ask her the other questions, Mrs. Mallory stopped the nurse and reminded her that she had had the same interview the week before. "Use the same procedure that you used for Tony Davis, who died here a week ago," she told her. She then walked back to the cubicle where Dave was, gently closed his eyes, and stayed with his body until it was removed from the hospital.

"A death and a funeral...all in the same week... in the same household! Who would have thought it would happen to me? Never in my life!" She inhaled slowly and EXHALED as she drove away from Mercy. "What am I going to do now?" she asked herself. "Should I delay Tony's funeral and have the two together? No, that's not an option. Tony's wake is in a few hours. It's too late to delay. I am going to have to bury Tony as scheduled and then arrange Dave's funeral later." She told herself..

Thinking that it would free her arrested nerves and allow her to feel something – pain, sadness, fear, blame, anything, Mrs. Mallory inhaled slowly a deep breath again and EXHALED FORCEFULLY again. But, the breathing exercise did not work. She remained a zombie void of emotions and robbed of the very substance that gave her life – her son, her husband, and by the end of Dave's funeral her job... all gone.

As planned, she went to her son's wake that night and managed to attend the funeral the next day. She did not breakdown or cry out in sorrow as she had done when she tried to arrange her son's service. And to her surprise, she had no problems planning her husband's funeral the next day.

"Set the funeral for next Saturday. I am going to skip the wake service," Mrs. Mallory told the secretary. "Oh by the way, there is no need to view the body before Saturday. I trust that you will give my husband the same caring service that you gave my son." With that said, she selected their prime funeral package as casually as a bride would select a wedding dress. But unlike with the bride there was no joy in her heart. For, her feelings – all of them – were dead.

During the days before the funeral, when she should have been so depressed that she needed bed rest, she went about her chores as usual. And, when a caring relative offered a Valium (as neighbors commonly did in Greenville when they thought you were depressed) to calm her nerves, she refused it declaring that she was fine. On the Wednesday night before the funeral she went to play bingo. When her weekly competitor noticed her there, some said among themselves, "Mrs. Mallory is either crazy, or she cares nothing for husband and son." Others were suspicious of a little foul play in the Davis's family. And, these – talking close enough and loud enough – made sure that she heard their suspicions. But, if they were trying to push her into some kind of confrontation with them, they failed. Instead, Mallory became strangely detached from all her surroundings, and through her eyes all the players appeared vague, wavering but mocking stick figures which were too weak to incite her to rage or too cold to quick her numbness. At that moment, she slowly began to lose all sense of reality.

By the morning of Dave's funeral, Mallory was completely insane. No, she was not schizophrenic or manic-depressive, she was psychotic in that she saw "things." Things like post- death visions... the kind people have of their loved one right after the deceased's death. She saw Tony and Dave as plain as if they were still alive. When she woke that mornings and went into the kitchen to cook breakfast, Dave was there making her favorite, ham and eggs, and Tony was sitting at the table with his plate ready, waiting to eat as he had done when he was 5 or 6 years old. They tried to tell her something, but they disappeared before she understood the message. When she went to the bedroom to shower, Dave, already dressed in a black suit, urged her to hurry. "If you don't hurry, you are going to be late for my funeral," he told her." When the limousine came for her to take her to the funeral, Tony was the driver.

"I need to tell you something," he told her. But, before he did, he changed into Crain's regular driver and did not appear anymore that day.

"That's it," she said. "As soon as the funeral is over I'm checking myself into the hospital."

True to her word, she went to Mercy's outpatient clinic after the service, and when she told the doctor that she was seeing ghosts of her son and husband who had died within the last two weeks, he told her that he was going to transferred her to Mercy's Hospital emergency. "I don't think that I need emergency care. I'm just stressed," she protested. But, he transferred her anyway. And, she went to Mercy Hospital and checked into the ER.

The doctor and nurse on call were the same doctor and nurse that had seen her husband and son when they were in emergency. What a coincident, she thought... mother, father, and son... at the same emergency room with the same doctor and nurse. Little did she know that what was about to happen to her was far from coincidental.

"Nurse, strap Mrs. Mallory to the bed. Roll her into the holding cubicle," the doctor told her. "I'll prepare the... the... sedative." He said smiling as he unlocked the door that housed their secret – a Thanatron... their personal suicide machine.

When the doctor came into the cubicle carrying the machine, Mallory asked him, "What is that?"

"Glad you asked! I guess I can tell you since you won't be able to tell anyone else. This is a suicide machine, the same one that I used on your son and your husband"

"What are you talking about? My husband died of a heart attack and my son committed suicide."

"That's what you think. The truth is your husband survived his heart attack, and after your son's stomach was pumped, he was as good as new. Your son probably wouldn't have died if he'd sold the drugs like we tried to get him to do. But, no he tried to commit suicide...the easy way out... and he played right into our hands."

"Are you telling me that you killed them?" Mrs. Mallory asked as she tossed trying to free herself.

"Be still! You will only make thing worse!" The doctor shouted as he grabbed her arms and held her still. "Not only did we kill them, but we are the one that caused you to lose your job."

"What we?" Mrs. Mallory asked feeling her nerves again... tossing trying to free herself and unable to understand how people could be so inhuman.

"The paramedics, the coroner, the receptionist here in the emergency room, the pathologist that performs the autopsy, and even your superintendent who is our Grand Dragon: we are all members of the Klan. And, we are determined to stomp you niggers out just like we would roaches."

"The Klan... stomp us out..." Mrs. Mallory couldn't believe what she was hearing. She thought the Klan had disappeared from Greenville and Riverside in the 1980s. Never in a thousand years did she think that they would be a threat in 2014. But she felt her life in danger and cried out: "Help! Help! Help! Somebody help me!"

Just as the nurse was about to give her the fatal injections, the police stormed into the emergency room and into the cubicle. They seized the doctor and nurse, handcuffed them, and left almost as fast as they had come. However, before they left the emergency, Mallory heard a policeman say, "The next time you try to kill someone in the holding cubicle, make sure your turn off the intercom system."

. Thankfully, the security guard heard everything and summoned the police in time for them to stop another murder in the Davis family.

Unstrapped from her prison bed and moved to a room on main the floor, Mallory was given a routine exam. The only thing wrong with her was high blood pressure. "If your pressure goes any higher, you are going to have a stroke." The floor nurse told her. "We are going to have to keep you overnight to try to stabilize you. And, about those visions… you were under extreme stress because of your loss. Hopefully, when your pressure is down and you are de-stressed, they will go away. No, you are not insane," she assured her. "I have read that it's common for people to see or even hold conversations with the newly deceased. Maybe they were trying to tell you that they were murdered."

It was not easy getting her pressure down to normal. But finally, after five days, Mallory's nerves settled, and her pressure dropped below the danger zone. She was released and went home… to an empty house. She tried to get back to normal. But, for her… there was no normal. Her entire life had changed forever… just because of hate. She felt Dave and Tony's presence in the house, but she never saw them again after the day of the funeral. And, as time drifted away from that horrific chapter in her life, the nearness to them seemed further and further apart.

One day, after job hunting, Mallory stopped by The Catfish House for lunch. When she looked up from saying grace, Skeeter, the student whom she had not seen since that time at Chevron, was standing near her table. "Well, well, well," she said. "Skeeter, how are you? It's been a while"

"It sure has, Mrs. Mallory. It sure has…I am doing okay, now. But, for a while my conscience bothered me so much.

I couldn't stop drinking. I want you to know that am so sorry about what dey did to you. I wanted to tell you that you were blackballed by the Klan… I guess I was a coward –afraid for my own life. Believe me; my conscience done whipped me good for it."

"What are you talking about?"

"Remember, when you seen me the last time. You was pumping gas at Chevron, and I was drunk. I tried to tell you den that the Klan was coming ater you and yo family because you were doin' so good. But, I jist couldn't. Too much of a coward… I don't understand how some people can have so much hate in dem… still dey pretended to be such Christians plotting their evil in the church. Sometimes I look at sinners, and I look at Christians and dey all look the same. A person can't hardly tell dem apart, now a days. Really, a person jist can't believe his own eyes. If you live a hunderd years and some mo, don't you never forgit it. Don't you never forgit it."

About the Author

GLORY S. DAVIS is a retired educator with more than 40 years of experience in teaching English language arts, literature, and speech. A native of Louisiana, she is a graduate of Grambling State University of Grambling, Louisiana and Southeastern Louisiana University of Hammond, Louisiana. She holds a Master's Degree in Education and a National Board Certification in English Language Arts and Literature.

Since her retirement, Ms. Davis has devoted her time to writing, public speaking, and teaching Bible Study. She presently resides in rural Southeastern Louisiana and is the mother of two sons, Thomas L. Davis and Terry K, Jefferson.

Look for her next books inspired by her Christian faith:

Outside the Gates
Escape for Mothers of Prisoners